CHILD OF TRUE LOVERS

A STORY AND BEYOND

CHILD OF TRUE LOVERS

A STORY AND BEYOND

By

AYUSHI SINGH

MyBooks Publication
a brand of DigiConv Technologies Services Pvt. Ltd.

MyBooks Publication
publish@my-books.in

Paperback ISBN: 978-93-88282-18-5
eBook ISBN: 978-93-88282-19-2

About the Author

Read, as it can heal...

Read, although it's an illusion...but it hold the answers...

That the Reality don't!

Ayushi Singh (1992-Present) was born in Allahabad, India. Being an Indian writer she is well versed with languages like English and Hindi. Her first publication was **'In The Canopy of Life'** which is the compilation of short stories and poems, revealing various realms of life.**'Ehsaason Ka Ashiyana'** is her another Hindi Anthology where she has contributed as the co-author along with other four remarkable authors from the world of Hindi Literature. The name of her creation is, **'Nasamajh he Sahi'**.

Engineer at heart and Science being her major field of study she was always inclined to Human Psychology and Philosophy since she started writing. She believes that every problem could be solved if the thought process is altered. This creation is based on her true experience and is few of those which she created after thorough study.

Inclined towards Music she is also a guitarist and vocalist. Apart from this she is a versatile speaker and hosted many national and international shows.

Every Entertainer might be an Artist,

but every Artist is definitely not an Entertainer.

A true Artist could burn away that veil while you stand naked by the mirror ...

of which you were always afraid of .

Ayushi

Ayushi is an optimistic soul whose power lies in her voice and wisdom lies in her pen.

Dedicated to

My Grandparents

Late Shri. Anirudh Singh

Late Smt. Prabhavati

Late Shri Anand Prakash

Smt Sarla

&

My Parents

Mr. Anai Pratap Singh (Papa)

Dr. Indu Singh (Maa)

Vidushi (Sister)

and to all those people who shattered me so much
that now I can scatter my charm in the whole
Universe!

Lastly and Mostly ...

YOU...

for holding the tangible part of my soul!

In the Memory of Chauhan Sahab

Moolchand Chauhan
(1 September 1979 - 28 May 2018)

The only time goodbyes hurt is when you know there will never be a hello again.

The song may be over, but the melody will linger on.

~May Your Soul, Rest in Peace~

Preface

God is the ultimate icon of power and our parents are equivalent to Gods!

There is no doubt in this statement, however, being mortals they are also equally prone to mistakes like any of us. For us, they tried and are still trying their best to fulfill all that we need and desire for. Being their child, we are not obliged to doubt their skills in bringing us up, however, in spite of so much there is always a gap between their understanding and ours. Maybe because of the generation gap or thought process at a certain age, that we are not able to understand them and they are not able to understand us equally.

It's very true that we are **made** by our parents, however, **created** by our own choices and aspirations and no one and nothing else. Like me or anyone else, you are also an individual entity with much difference from what you carry from your family. Your choices, habits, and thoughts might not match with your family and that is totally natural. You are an isolated soul and your existence, survival and growth depend on the choices you make. No strings attached!

This novel is about the story of a child who is born to True Lovers. Accept it or not we all are inclined towards the genre 'Romance' and the ultimate climax could have only two cases and they are either a happy ending where the couple gets married and stays together forever or the sad ending and that could be isolation and despair. *The end of any story is never an ultimate conclusion but its an end of the particular phase as life keeps on moving till we cease to exist.*

The content of this book is based on my real life story, however, the characters names are changed. I am thankful to my parents (**Mr. Anai Pratap Singh & Dr. Indu Singh**) who supported me all through and made me capable enough to become the person I always wanted to be. I am also highly obliged to my little sister, **Vidushi** for her continuous motivation and support. She is the only soul on earth who knows me more than anyone else. She has lived those moments with me as we share many things like thought process and of course our parents.

I will not forget to mention the names of **Divya Di** and **Manish Kumar** with whom I got the idea to draft this book. The seed of this book was already sown when one of my close friends **Kartikey Singh** motivated me to write a novel with a liberal heart and not a business mind. A great suggestion though! Well my another friend from Chennai, **Ronak Talreja** was no less a foundation for this novel. With his regular criticism, I was able to create the best draft of this book. I will never forget to mention the names of my friends **Soham Banerjee, Rahul Kumar, Rahul Yadav, Bidur Narayan, Shashi Verma, Pooja Gupta, Sunayna Chaudhary, Shubham Semwal, Ujjwal Bajaj, Komal Kansal, Aarti, Pammi, Shivani Shakya, Sparna Saxena, Mayank Agarwal, Kusum Jangra, Anjali Giri, Nandan Kumar, Vishwa Ajit Singh, Sonu Thakur, Sunil Pandey Ji and Ankit Porwal** who bestowed faith in me to be a successful writer.

Being a social person, it is very difficult to mention every name whom I owe my life and career for being at this position, however, I will try to cover it accordingly like my childhood friends, pals from St. Mary's Convent Allahabad and Sharda University Greater Noida, Colleagues from HCL, Infosys, Cognizant, Network Bulls, Radicle Inc and many of my Pg mates and Hostlers in Chennai, Mysore, Gurgaon, and Noida.

Well, the list is still not ended, as there are many people who taught me unknowingly. They were strangers and I don't know their names however their teachings are engraved deep in my heart.

I also want to mention the names of my uncles **Dr. Anuj Singh and Shri Lalla Singh** who are great teachers and father figures.

Hardly anyone will disagree with the fact that if a person is not a support then a lesson. I will also convey my gratitude to all my critics who helped me to take their criticism as the challenge and conquer every hurdle that had been an obstacle while the creation of this novel.

While creating this novel I lost a very significant person of my life **Mr. Moolchand Chauhan** (known by Chauhan Sahab) who was not only my publisher but also my friend and guardian. He was a pious soul with a jovial heart. He possessed the charm to make anyone smile. Even in this critical phase his wife **Mrs. Kusum Chauhan** and his business partner and Managing Director of My Books Publication, **Mr. Shahid Khan** stood up and guided me through the whole publication process. Thank you Team!

The world is a large place, larger than our imagination and our lifetime duration is negligible and an impossible time duration to know and touch each aspect of it. Well, the internet is helping us reach many. In the process of creation of this book, practically I met none, however virtually I came to know that there are people like me who were having the same experiences as discussed in the book. I want to thank **Ian Wilson** and **Tipharot** for their wonderful explanation of precognitive dreams on their youtube channels. I also want to thank the **Institute of Noetic Science** channel for their influential content.

I am not sure whether this token of gratitude will ever reach her/him who was once the contributor of HuffPost Contributor platform which is no more active. Although I have found many contents on schizophrenia and precognitive dreams this content was so realistic and relatable that it brought goosebumps. **Thank You** very much dear writer for that content. I was very fortunate to read that.

While going through hundreds of content online I also met **Michael and Susan Schofield** who were having two kids with the rare disese of Schizophrenia. That was a really hard time for them. After watching the video I realized that mental illness is a curse for not only the patients but their loved ones too. The process from diagnosis to medication requires a lot of suffering and patience especially when the patient is your own kid.

I want to extend my gratitude to **Psychologist Jeffrey Mishlove and Dr. Edie C May who is the Director of Military Intelligence Psychic and Spying program (Project Stargate)** for making me understand the science behind the occurrence of Precognitive dreams.

I am grateful to you that you are holding the tangible part of my soul! This book is solely based on my words and expressions with an intention to bring about liberal thinking in society and about choices anyone makes in life. Be it any element, career, person, path or religion.

This book is not a love story but a story beyond with my observations and experiments with reality.

This book is ME!

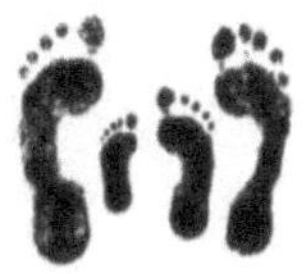

Contents

...Before you start

So if you are a rigid personality i.e you are stubborn with your ideas, beliefs, and thoughts then this book might not be the right choice for you as it consists of those theories and facts that you might find contradicting. You might turn judgmental which will end up in contradicting thoughts and assumptions. Being the creator of this novel I will not appreciate that .

This creation is a blend of a thorough study and practical experience. You are free to make judgments, but only after you read the whole creation. (and of course with a liberal mind). However, if you cling to a particular thought, idea, experience, belief or philosophy, you will not be able to go further.

Disclaimer: The content of this book is based on real experiences and if you are skeptical about those thoughts, ideas or experiences then you can continue to be one as the author is not trying to sell anything, convince or thrust her ideas on you.

A liberal heart, open mind and soul with a vision is best suited for this creation.

A Brief Thought:

Theoretically, words are just expressions.
Practically they are swords and poison or Bliss and Medicine.

The more we say that we don't judge by words but actions, the more we lie to ourselves.

We judge by what we perceive in the first place and there is NO exception to that. Now before I move ahead, I would like to ask you…

For you, what is a judgment?

Well, according to the dictionary definition:

'Judgement is the ability to make considered decisions or come to sensible conclusions.'

According to me, **a judgment is a conclusion that we make by putting our knowledge and expressions in the equation which we frame by ourselves. Now, how does this guarantee that the database of our knowledge is enough or the equation we framed is correct?**

The answer to this is very critical and too hard for us to accept. As we grow we become so rigid in our choices, values, and morals that we are not ready to accept life as it is. And maybe that could be the reason it is said, God created a Child and not Man! A man is created by just handful experiences that he had in his lifetime. His curiosity vanishes with time and he lives in a world created by himself where he thinks he makes the most 'logical' choices and decisions.

On the frequency of occurrence of any event, we start predicting things so frequently that when we fail in our predictions we start complaining God and Luck (Few of Our favorite words which we use frequently!) And here the universal fact upholds saying that it is always easy to write on a Blank Blackboard than writing on the one which is already scribbled!

So it's always best to live with the attitude of ACCEPTANCE!

Well, too much philosophy on the first few pages right? You might be wondering if this is the start then what will be the rest of the content?

Well...then grab your coffee and drag your attention as here I want to confess that this work of mine is not highly philosophical! It is REAL! We all are philosophers but the true philosophical part is dormant because we use more of probabilistic techniques than philosophical, as a result, we end up making the wrong choices. And by 'wrong choices', I mean those choices which make us unhappy.

"My body may turn into ashes and my soul will wander helpless or maybe change its spiritual path but this piece of art will stay forever in some faded pages for years to come."

- Ayushi Singh

HAPPY READING!

Chapter 1

The Introduction

Principle of Causality

The effect of an event cannot occur before it's occurrence.

In other words, every event give rise to another and they cannot occur independently. Scientists claim that there could be no ripple in the ocean unless there is a strong force hitting the surface of the water or some commotion below the surface. This principle strongly negates the existence of predictions or what we can say precognition.

Well, that is theory and theories are created to study and bring a conclusion according to the probability of their occurrence. That doesn't guarantee, accuracy. Does it?

The Science behind the Second Sight

Second Sight is a term that is not much found on the internet as it's a part of pseudoscience. And pseudoscience is all about beliefs on experiences which may contradict the existing laws of Science.

According to the definition, "Second Sight is a form of extrasensory perception, the supposed power to perceive things that are not present to the senses, whereby a person perceives information, in the form of a vision, about future events before they happen (precognition), or about things or events at remote locations (remote viewing)".

Precognition and Retro Cognition

Precognition, also called prescience, future vision, future sightings an alleged psychic ability to see events in the future. As with other forms of extrasensory perception, there is no reliable scientific evidence that precognition is a real ability possessed by anyone and it is widely considered to be pseudoscience. Specifically, precognition appears to violate the principle of causality, that an effect cannot occur before it's cause.

Well, as mentioned prior there is no strong theory defined for this.

You might be thinking why I have mentioned these terminologies at the beginning of the book. And if you are a person who is not much into science then you might end up accusing me for using these hefty terminologies in the very beginning of the book. Well, this book is all about these scientific terms which can be broadly categorized under **Pseudoscience**.

What is Pseudoscience?

Pseudoscience consists of statements, beliefs, or practices that are claimed to be both scientific and factual but are incompatible with the scientific method.

We cannot believe and rely on Science totally as we all know that Science is still unable to prove the existence of God. Everything is power and there are miracles and unnatural events too.

Having knowledge of the future is great but obviously knowing the future which could not be altered whatsoever is quite absurd. Astrologers are the people who can easily alter our minds and their words that can actually affect us. But what if we could see future incidents without any external effort, person or force?

The repeated flashes and reflections of pasts or future can haunt anyone. It's more absurd than it sounds. To many of us it may sound like a superpower but believe me, it is not. We have been jested with only those capabilities which we can handle well. Knowing or having more might not always be good for our existence.

Taking a very simple example from the real world... why we often believe that everyone cannot be a leader. Do you know why?

Well, the person may not be able to handle power and start misusing it. There are many cases from the history that claim and portray few figures justifying the statement. When any irrelevant power is thrust on someone it may deeply affect his physical and mental being, as a result, they may end up making the wrong decisions.

Chapter 2

An Absolute Love Story

Never lose your wildness. Never doubt your choices.

Your wisdom with help you to choose the best and your passion will help you to keep it safe, unharmed … forever.

I have not read much about Romeo Juliet, Heer Ranjha or Laila Majnu but I have seen and lived with Aadir and Ira and I am Pretty sure they were no less. This story falls within the timeline of the 20th-century end and 21st-century start.

Aadir and Ira had an incredible love story. A love story that everyone dreamt of. A story of passion and commitment which was built on a very strong foundation of trust. If you are an Indian and in love then you might have to put in some extra efforts to make your relationship work. Either you have to convince people or get convinced for yourself. The choice is always in your hand.

Ira was truly devoted to Aadir however when it came to commitment and moving the relationship to the next level of marriage, Aadir was little doubtful as he had family responsibilities. There was also one biggest hurdle and that is often the only reason for numerous 'mutual' breakups in Indian Marriages and that was caste and religion variation.

Sometimes I feel that we all should create a standard logo of each religion and caste and get it tattooed on our 'foreheads' and accordingly we should fall in love (as those tattoos will be clearly visible on our faces) maybe that could make our lives hassle-free. Well, then too I doubt that this will work as our society my not accept the fact that *we choose* our soul mates. I agree that the thought process is changing in the society but the change is too slow to be noticed.

If we all are the victims of society then who is the society?

The solution to this is the day when we stop meddling in others affairs or stop judging them then our 'society' will also improve, tremendously.

Ira was a Ph.D. scholar with her majors in Thermodynamics. A very charming personality and a heart full of wisdom. Her strong moral and spiritual inclination was an inspiration to many. Thick dark hair and beautifully carved personality made other girls feel envious of her. Her features were so sharp that it resembled with the beauty of South Indian girls. A perfect blend of brains and beauty.

On the other hand, Aadir was a tall and fair guy with a humorous mind and pure heart. Fuming black curly hairs with a strongly built personality clearly reflected that he possessed the genes of Aryans. Girls of his college had a major crush on him however he lost his heart and soul to someone else.

Ira and Aadir studied in the same University. An ambitious attitude with many dreams to fulfill was their first common characteristic. Loyalty towards relationships and strong moral values were the next two. Although they had the same thought process, however, the way to express was very different. Ira was soft and calm whereas Aadir was just the contrast.

Another element that varied was their upbringings. Aadir lost his mother when he was seven due to this he always had a soft corner and desires for family love. Although he had a huge joint family, however, being the youngest, he was not able to enjoy the family quality time as all the elder siblings were married and busy with their family duties.

On the other hand, Ira was a typical family girl as she was brought up in a typical joint family. She was a darling to her parents and siblings. Being very close to her father, she shared everything with him. So did Aadir.

They both studied together and as we all know, thatage is very tender. They fell in love. Their fragrance of love was obvious to spread. So it did.

The first person to realize that we are in Love is most of the time our best friends. This time was no exception!

Veer was Aadir's bestie and roomie. He felt something fishy and made Aadir speak out the truth. Well, his doubt was a truth. He was more than happy to know and be a part of this love story.

Veer, Aadir, and Ira were pursuing their post-graduation, and at that age, the maturity level is quite high as compared to teenagers. There was nothing like 'timepass' in their relationship. They were utterly serious about it. However, realizing the level of commitment and giving it the name of marriage scared Aadir. On the other hand, Ira was adamant to marry, Aadir.

Being the favorite daughter of her father, Ira confessed her love to him and made him absolutely clear that she will get married to Aadir or none. Mr. Rai was a very genuine person. He realised the intensity of his daughter's love and never forced her to marry anyone else. He accepted the fact that Ira was a well educated independent lady and she could live her life on her own choices and rules. Similarly, Aadir gave a hint to his father about Ira and his feelings for her.

Most of us might have experienced that if we are deeply attached to someone, we can feel their sorrow or pain when they are far apart. Similarly, whenever anything grave happened to Aadir, Ira felt the vibes of it. I would not say a very absolute picture of it but yes something relatable.

This sounds absurd, right? Well, you can ask your parents or someone very close to you. They might have felt something similar for you or maybe you might have felt for someone. It's a proven scientific fact. Being specific this could be broadly categorized under a scientific term **Telepathy**. Also, emotions play a major role here.

Telepathy is the purported transmission of information from one person to another without using any known human sensory channels or physical interaction.

There are very few scientific evidences to prove that but just because we have fewer theories or no scientists claiming it's existence we cannot deny that it does exist.

It was a common day but very uncommon thing was about to happen. College sessions was about to end when Aadir's father had a paralytic attack. This news was a setback to Aadir as Mr. Solanki was the only parent he was left with. Losing parents is equally painful as losing your child. It was Mr. Solanki's dream to see his youngest son settled before he dies.

However, fate had something else stored for him. His sudden illness turned Aadir's life upside-down. He decided to leave the town and go back to his hometown to help his father in recovery, but before that he wanted a last visit with Ira.

When Ira came to know about Mr. Solanki's illness then she got all the answers to her uneasiness since last few days. Because of examinations, she was not able to communicate with either Aadir or Veer, however, something was continuously bugging her and she was unaware of it. That was Mr. Solanki's illness.

After explaining her the reason why he is leaving to his village he spoke the words he never wanted to. "I may never come back, Ira!"

"I will wait!" - Ira's calm voice reverted with the answer.

With these words, they departed. Understanding the seriousness of the situation, neither Aadir explained nor does Ira asked for an explanation.

Months went by and there was no news from Aadir. On the other hand, Mr. Rai was getting worried about Ira as she was already settled in her career and now it was her turn to get married among all her siblings.

One day, he decided to have this conversation with his daughter which he tried to avoid for long.

It was a rainy day when Ira was sipping her coffee in the balcony by her room. Water was dripping off the edges of roof and sometimes made way into her cup but Ira was too engrossed in her thoughts to notice.

After Aadir departed, Ira used to stay alone, pondering and staring at the infinity of sky. Her endless thoughts and unanswered questions made her secluded. She started avoiding family functions or gatherings. Mr. Rai could sense that very well.

"Ira, are you still waiting for Aadir to come back and marry you?"

A husky but calm voice alarmed Ira and when she turned back she saw her father standing, with never-ending questions in his small yet vibrant eyes.

"Hey, Dad, when you came here? I never noticed you! Do you want to have some coffee?" interrupted Ira with reverse questioning.

Mr. Rai noticed her swollen eyes with eyeballs floating in the water. The reason was obvious. He repeated his question in the same tone. To this she replied, "Dad, I never expect anything from him however if my love is true and pious, he will have to return". The conversation was ended with her last statement. Mr. Rai realised that he should not bother her for some time.

On the other hand, the storm in Aadir's life settled but took Mr. Solanki along with it. Aadir was shattered by his father's death. The only person who was with him throughout was his best friend Veer.

Last words of Mr. Solanki to Aadir were:

"Whatever you do in your life Son, but never betray a true heart. The scream of that broken heart will shatter your mansion of Wealth or Prosperity, howsoever strong it's foundation is."

At that moment, only one thought came to Aadir's mind and he pledged to marry Ira!

After his father's demise he went to his other family members for the support and approval but they all were so much busy in their lives and society that they were not able to see his intense love for Ira. Only his father could, who was no more with him.

They offered him either to get married to the girl of their choice or abandon the family. Aadir was stuck! It was a very difficult decision for an orphan who was only left with his siblings to choose between family and love.

At-last Aadir chose LOVE.

It requires a lot of guts for a shattered, family-less and unemployed boy to stand for his love who has no clue of his future. Aadir did that. His risk-taking attitude surprised many. After trying hard to convince his family members and realizing that he cannot succeed, Aadir abandoned his family. He told the whole scenario to Veer and as expected, Veer was always ready to risk anything for Aadir. So they decided to meet Mr. Rai with a proposal of marriage.

You can never feel more special than when your prayers are answered! Ira was so exuberated with happiness that she could not hold back her tears. Aadir was jobless and family-less when he put forth the proposal of marriage which was not acceptable to Ira's mother and other family members. This was obvious however, Mr. Rai was assured of Aadir's capability and proud of his daughter's choice.

On the pious day of Maha-Shivratri, Aadir and Ira were officially declared Man and Wife.

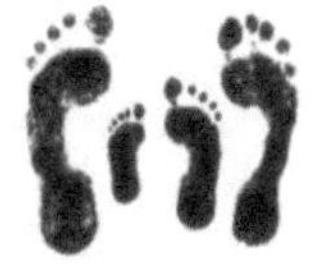

Chapter 3

The Toddler

"…like trying to paint the perfect sunset, I could never write You, as perfectly as You are already written"

-Matthew Spenser

Ambition and Loyalty were the two major similarities between Ira and Aadir. They both were equally devoted to their careers as they were to each other. Aadir was from the northern part of India where the designation of IAS (Indian Administrative Service) was considered the top-notch career option and nothing lower can suffice to call you 'Successful'. A typical guy with a rural background and low exposure to worldly affairs was told that IAS is the only definition of success in life and nothing else.

Whereas, Ira was brought up in a well-equipped family where girls were not expected much to excel in education. The only expectation that their family members had from themselves were to fetch the best grooms compatible with their daughter's personalities.

The best term that could define Aadir was *diligence*. He used to study very hard to excel in education that even today, I am uncertain about a story (was a myth or truth) about his eyes which became permanently reddish (during his college days) as the veins of the eyeballs popped up because of enormous strain and multiple sleepless nights.

In spite of being the treasure of knowledge, he lacked communication skills which were quite necessary to crack the PI rounds in the IAS exams. He cleared all the theory papers which were the hardest nut to crack however his IAS PI exam due date coincided post seven days his father's death. He got very less time to prepare as a result he failed in the same. Aadir's IQ level was unquestionable however he lacked communication skills. Communication was the major reason of his failure. On that particular day, he pledged that he will raise his child making communication and language as it's major strength.

On the other hand Ira got an opportunity to study in IIT Mumbai for her Ph.D. and further research, however, she chose love over career and declined the offer.

Aadir and Ira were highly intellectual individuals. From career to solving life problems, their approach was commendable. They as a couple were an inspiration to many as together they struggled to build the mansion of their dreams. No wedding presents or any financial or family support. They only had their qualifications and a small apartment on rent. It is a big decision for a father to get her highly qualified daughter married to the guy who was unemployed and had no family. However, Mr. Rai was a very sorted person who had deep faith in Aadir's caliber.

You are empowered when your parents believe in what you believe!

Yes... Mr. Rai and Mr. Solanki were the ideal examples in this story.

Their life was limited when they were married. Limited clothes, food, and other resources. Although they had very strong family backgrounds, they chose self-respect and determined in building their own mansion of dreams.

Aadir and Ira were overqualified for any jobs that were offered to them however they chose them to make through for survival. At times Aadir used to feel low when he saw his friends working at a higher designation than he does. As he felt hopeless, Ira used to console him saying... *'We will make through it! Believe me!'*

They worked through thick and thin and when economic conditions were stable they ultimately planned a baby. One year later, I was born!

It was a hot silent night of May 15th, when at about 11:45 pm Dr. Pramila came running to Aadir informing that he was blessed with a girl child but unfortunately she was not responding. She claimed that the newborn was required to be monitored in child ventilator or else they might lose her. The worst news was, there were no child ventilators available in that hospital. The other hospital was about at a distance of fifteen minutes.

Each new second was a new challenge for her. She could have collapsed anytime but... maybe...

She had faith her father's faith!

In that fraction of second, Aadir suffered strange fluctuation of emotions from very happy to extremely nervous.

"I cannot afford to lose her, She is all that I have!" Aadir cried looking at the tiny eyes who were struggling to open.

Anyhow he, along with a relative reached the hospital and then the newborn was put under the supervision of a senior doctor. That day of birth was a little difficult for the family but the days after that were no less challenging.

After she entered the world, Aadir and Ira started to dream big. Their expectations started increasing. They named her, Sarah.

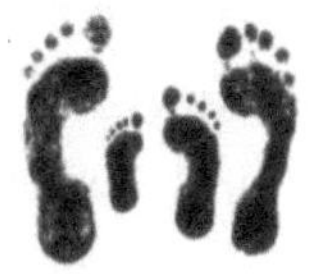

Chapter 4

The Journey Begins!

Open up your eyes, Little One .

Conquer your fear and self doubt.

You don't have to see the whole mountain, to begin this treacherous climb.

As you move along each mile, I promise you will figure it out.

Sarah was a chubby little girl with dark brown eyes and neatly shaped lips. Whosoever saw her said that she resembled her dad. Well, why not, she was his princess. Round face with popping eyes and fuming black hairs were alluring. She didn't cry when she was born. She came to this world silently.

Unlike many kids Sarah, spoke less and observed more. And, like any other parents, Aadir and Ira left no stone unturned to bring the best for her. *She was the rich princess of poor parents.* As she grew, the expenditure of the family rose drastically. But we all know that when we have the power of Love we can conquer mountains. Both started working harder and time started changing. Aadir believed that Sarah was the reason behind that change! He considered her the 'Lucky Charm' of their little world.

Be it any fair or occasion, Aadir always took her along. She was the best thing happened to him. Any neighbor or relative would always find Sarah clinging to her father. Ira, on the other hand, acted a little mature and started focusing on future plans like Sarah's education. She decided to give home tuitions so that she can accumulate enough money for Sarah's future.

As Sarah grew, Ira observed few characteristics that were developing in Sarah which were a little different from other children. Sarah never crawled or trotted on her knees, she directly walked on her feet. Also, she started memorizing music pieces easily as compared to the pronunciation of words. There were few music tracks when she used to respond to even if she was deeply unconscious in sleep.

After asking few medical practitioners she came to know that Sarah's brain was always hyper active and could quickly perceive and respond to the minute details in the environment.

This was all told to me by my mother!

My first school was 'Magic Years Nursery' a small school in the neighborhood. That was the first place where I learned the Universal Poem, 'Twinkle Little Star' which gradually became my favorite. The musical track of this poem was what I grasped earlier than the lyrics.

It is said that mothers are more intuitive than fathers, well in this case too my mother proved to be better than dad in observing me. She observed that I get influenced deeply and very easily by the environment, events, and people.

A very popular incident in my family history took place in the year 1994 when I was about three years old. We all were watching India's blockbuster movie 'DDLJ' on television. I was so much engrossed and taken away by the character Raj that I started imitating that character. I am unsure if I could remember the plot of the movie but I was sure that the character Raj influenced me a lot. I had a toy guitar and it became my only best friend.

Day and night I used to roam around with that guitar clinging to me and singing 'Tujhe Dekha To Ye Jana... (Title Track of DDLJ). I started doubting my personality. Whosoever would ask me "What is your Name?" My answer would always be "Shahrukh Khan"! Wasn't that funny? This characteristic is often seen in kids. At the tender age of 3-5, they start imitating their superheroes or any influential member in the family. Shaktiman was another childhood hero of that era where kids used to imitate his style. I choose SRK.

If it was just a playful act then this could have been considered very natural but I started doubting my personality. Switching characters for me was becoming difficult. So I started considering myself SRK.

My mother observed everything and it was obvious that she was worried. However, she was told that the age group of 3-5 years and those crazy things were the normal combination and, realizing that she started to take things lightly.

For a mediocre family, it is always difficult to get their child admitted to Convent Schools. However, Aadir was adamant to get Sarah admitted in Convent. He wished his daughter should ace the domain in which he failed and that was English Communication.

Like an ideal father, he brought the entrance application to get me admitted there.

I was trotting around when I saw mom was talking to my dad.

"What form is this?" Inquired Ira.

"Admission form of St. Mary's Convent!", replied Aadir.

"But you know it is a very expensive school, we cannot afford to get her admitted there. And apart from that, the selection process is not easy….and.."

On this Aadir took a deep breath and sat beside Ira and said, "Yes Ira, getting her admitted and the fees structure is another level question, first we need to get her clear the rounds of selection!". After a pause, he said, "Let us at least try…".

Ira grasped my figures tightly as I was about to stumble from my favorite chair that my uncle gifted me on my last birthday, and said, "I will get her prepared."

And from that day, preparation began!

Convent Schools had a very complicated selection process. They had a separate selection process for parents, as well. Only educated guardians with a strong economic background could clear the selection rounds. Although they were not very strong economically, Aadir's and Ira's education qualification made the balls roll in the court.

I always believed that my parents got lesser than what they deserved! The reason was, they never asked for it!

My mother tried her best to make me mug up the spelling of my name S A R A H, however, it was difficult for me to believe that my name is something other than Shahrukh Khan! At that age, my mother realised that my perception skill was stronger than my memory. It was difficult for me to accept something that was told. I believed more on my perception.

I was weak with facts but great at imagination or you can say observation. My brain was hyperactive when it had to recognize colors. Blue, Velvet Blue, Persian Blue, Ink Blue, and what not...! But when it had to mug up poems, it failed.

At last, the day of my first interview came along with the worried faces of my parents.

Along with my parents, I entered the huge mansion of red bricks where people craved to get their daughters admitted, The St. Mary's Convent! I still remember the tensed look on my parent's face. I was dressed very well with a neatly tired pony and lilac frock which had a mild fragrance of lilies. I was not able to understand what was expected out of me.

An elderly woman entered the room wearing a white gown with a flowing white skirt on her head. Believe me, that was a great deal of distraction for me. Later on, I was told she was a Nun, and that skirt on the head was called 'Cornette'.

My parents were asked to wait outside while I was going to get grilled.

She looked at me with a smile on her face and asked a few questions. I cannot remember much, but when I strain my mind I could recall a rough conversation like this:

Nun: "Hello Dear! Good After Noon"

Me: "...Good... af... noon!"

She sounded very happy and excited.

Nun: "What is your name, Child?"

Me: "Shahrukh Khan"

...and that was how the disaster began.

On this I could not remember the exact expression of that Nun, however, I am sure, she was not happy but confused! She checked my application again and repeated the same question. My answer was the same. She switched to other questions which were about colors and alphabets!

I was sure I did very well in the whole interview session but never understood why my parents were not happy when I narrated the whole incident to them. I could have done better but which school will select a child who suffered an identity crisis?

I was not able to understand where I did wrong as I was very sure that all the answers related to colors and alphabets were absolutely correct.

On the day of result, my parents were feeling little jittery, still, there was a spark of hope left in my father's heart. I never believed in my luck but he always did. Although I was only five, I remember there was not much cheerfulness that day at home.

That little hope forced Aadir to step out of the house and go to the result center. Ira knew that she cannot stop Aadir to relinquish his inquisitiveness. With the perplexing mind storming with random thoughts he drove to the center. In great hustle bustle, he reached the soft board where the most awaited list of selected candidates was pinned.

144. Sarah Solanki 15182530

This name was shining amongst all! Aadir's intuition worked!

From a nearby public calling booth, he dialed to Ira.

"Ira, she made it and as you usually say... yes... we made through!", screamed Aadir, and burst out in tears!

Ira stood up and hugged me!

Battle was half Won.

Things may sound simple and easy but each little victory was celebrated in that family. So they did. I was not sure how I was selected when I told her the wrong name, maybe the reason could be my parents.

Well, I was very happy to see them happy without realizing the importance of that event.

Chapter 5

The Realization

There are nothing like 'rules' and 'routines' there are only 'incidents' and 'accidents'.

The first day of school is always an incredible memory to keep forever, however, I could not remember what exactly it was like to be in the school so renowned. I was too young to judge.

St. Mary's Convent was one of the highly credible schools in my city. It was basically for the 'High Class' society, however, sometimes 'Middle Class' individuals also struggled and got through the complex interview round that was conducted by the school. Well all these things were told to me by my so called 'Society' otherwise I am not used to words like 'High Class' or 'Low Class'.

St. Mary's Convent was the best decision of my parents for me. And I am highly thankful to them for giving me the best education in spite of struggling financially!

Neatly built old style the British Architecture, this building was standing still since the British came to India. Still so vibrant that it appeared as if it had a body of a teenage and wisdom of an adult. Renowned for it's preaching and education, any guardian would feel proud to send their kids to this school as the whole process from getting admitted to qualifying in the exam was unique and equally tough.

My twelve years in this school went somewhere in between Annual Days, Fests, Exams, Picnics, Lectures, Friendship, Tears, and Laughter. Disciplined life and good education were what we got from there.

There were few absurd habit's of mine which I observed over time like, I never played with dolls and never liked idols or paintings which were realistic, because when I observed too many things in one timeframe, my multiple imaginations overlapped as a result, things that might appear 'realistic' to you actually appeared 'real' to me. And that was scary.

I remember, there was a marble idol of Mother Mary Ward in my school which was lush white. So beautifully carved that I along with my friend used to visit that place regularly. We visited chapels too. I never liked the eerie silence there, however, believing that to be a pious place I started visiting regularly.

I was about thirteen when this absurd incident occurred.

I saw myself walking on the thick dark and lonely streets. While I was drifting in darkness I could see the same pillars and designs that were present in my school. The same structure, red bricks which were appearing gloomy at night as there was not a single soul other than me. I never understood why I was continuously walking towards that white marble statue of mother Mary Ward which I was scared of. I stood beneath it and suddenly a storm occurred and her cornette flew away with that strong blow of wind.

Damn! That chilled my veins and I was clueless about where should I escape from. The most horrifying scene was when her bald scalp was exposed.

It was a dream!

When I woke up from the dream I saw red patches below my left eye and on my neckline. It was itchy and when I touched it, it was warm and swollen.

Without telling anybody about my dream, I started preparing myself to go to school. I was very disturbed. Even after covering my face with a layer of baby powder, the red tint on my face was visible.

You can escape from the world but from Mom... Never! She found that tint on my face and asked me what happened. Even I was clueless, what exactly happened.

With the swollen left eye I went to school. No doubt it was absurd but I had not escape even after trying ice cubes or talc. When I entered the school, I thought I would be the center of attraction for everyone present there. Well, I was wrong! There was something else everyone was talking about. Death of Sister Christina! This was a disturbing announcement that Sister Christina expired.

Sister Christina was the principal of the SMC for many years. She was the same lady who interviewed me when I joined the school. Her persona was adorable. The whole school was moaning while I was staring at the shiny white marble statue which perturbed me in my sleep.

Generally, I don't relate things much but that incident left me very unhappy and disturbed. I opted not to discuss with anyone. From that day onwards, I changed my routes so as to avoid any encounter with that statue.

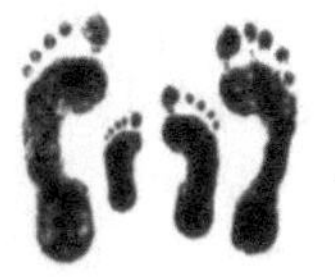

Chapter 6

The First Step

Don't downgrade your Dreams to match your Reality.

Upgrade your Belief to match your Vision!

I was an extremely quiet person who rarely spoke my heart out. However, my observations were very loud. I was always an observer than a speaker. I always accepted things or suggestions as they were. The only answer to every question for me was 'OKAY' because I never wanted to contradict or choose an option which needed explanation. I was always the majority section of the crowd even when I knew I never belonged there.

My mother was my inspiration and as she expected me to be, I was molded into a polite child. But in that process of molding, I turned very confused and lacked confidence. I was always doubtful and scared while taking any decision.

I was Sarah, the dull and under confidence child who was scared to interact, protest or even fight for herself. That was definitely not what my mother wanted me to be.

We lived in one of the poshest colonies of the city. Our neighbors had a higher standard of living. Their living style was much different from ours. I would not say that they were wealthier, however, I would frame this way, 'they could spend easily on things which might not be in their priority'.

I made few friends from the neighborhood or maybe friendship was thrust upon me. Piya and Mani were few of them. Piya was the smarter and wittier one. She had a dominating personality, however, I was always mute. Initially, I felt suffocating but then gradually I started accepting things as they were. I could be easily tamed. That was the reason I could easily fit in anything 'they' wanted me to be in. My sole existence was to increase the number of participants.

When I was about six, my uncle bought me a beautiful French doll with golden fringes and blue eyes. I never liked her. It appeared to me as if she was always staring at me. That made me uncomfortable. When my mother noticed that I tried to keep her away from me. She wanted to know the reason. When I told her the reason she framed it another way and told to me that the doll was not staring at me, she was just a little friend and needed to be taken care of. Well, that was not enough to convince me. Her glittering blue frock with the sheeny rubber skin was eye candy to many of my friends but definitely not me. I kept her away from me as I always knew she was staring at me, continuously!

One winter evening, Piya came to invite me at her home to play. While I was getting ready, she noticed my French doll and said 'Why don't you bring this doll along with us? We would cook some food for her too?' I had very limited toys however whenever anyone showed interest in that, I used to feel delighted! I took permission from my mother and went.

After three hours I returned home without the doll!

When my mother asked about the doll, I was clueless about what to say. When she gave me a stern look I told her that it was not my doll as Piya claimed that doll to be hers as she lost that same doll a few days ago.

At this explanation of mine, I am sure, my mother would have felt pity and angry at me at the same time. I was so fragile and confused that anyone could have manipulated me with almost no effort. Or maybe... I was always ignorant! This was a deep cause of worry for my mother.

A few days later, Piya's parents bought her a bicycle. Vibrant mauve colored with black stripes! It was beautiful indeed, however, she never allowed me to ride on that, so the maximum what I could do was, she rode while I chased her on foot!

My mother was always noticing me. Now she was scared of what I was turning into. Maybe I desired a bicycle, but never had the guts to ask for that from my parents. Or maybe I never realised what I wanted. After watching me chase Piya she turned so furious that she was determined to get me a new bicycle!

That was a dream come true for a fifteen-year-old Sarah.

Deep pink and freshly manufactured Lady Bird Bicycle turned into my pride. When I got my new friend, Piya realised that she lost me. So as a revenge she started puncturing the tires of my bicycle whenever I retired from riding. Each morning when I came to ride my bicycle, I had flattened tires!

I told this incident to my parents. This time my father stood up to sort the matter. Since he had an extremely intuitive mind, he solved the problem in a very smart and unexpected way.

My strange subservient nature was worrying my parents! What they expected me to be and what I was turning into. I was facing difficulty in decision making and expressing what I wanted.

When I got my bicycle I was facing another challenge (which I never discussed with anyone) and that was remembering routes. Whenever I rode outside the vicinity of my residence, I could not return back and find my way back home. I never told this to anyone but decided to find a solution to this problem on my own. However, even after multiple attempts, I failed.

Like any other child, I had more inclination towards music and dance than academics. I always wanted to participate in dance or music activities in my school however, my willingness and desires were not loud and clear enough to be heard. I was always hesitant or maybe fearful of rejection.

Maybe I knew I was lagging in many fields. It was not my introvert nature but it was something else. I was developing many weaknesses as I was growing up. The biggest one was to differentiate between imagination and reality. My thoughts and ideas were so loud, realistic and clear that I actually struggled to differentiate between reality and imaginations.

On any occasion, the smarter and outspoken classmates of mine got the opportunity to perform rather than me. I was always categorized in 'left out children' who were not having any specific talent, but according to the rules of school, had to participate in something or the other. As a result, I was always in the music band where we often found the 'left out kids' who were either not regular to school or were having no 'specific talent' and had 'stage fright'. I never expressed these things to my mother but deeply wished that one day I will perform all by myself.

I was disappearing in the crowd which I never wanted to but thought to be a better option than to be mocked at. I tried hard to claim my existence but failed because I lacked words. I was not able to portray myself to the people. As a result, I was ignored all the time.

According to human psychology research being ignored causes the same chemical reaction in the brain as experiencing a physical injury!

I had to find a way out!

I remember many incidents where I gathered courage to ask my teacher to perform in any event or annual days but I was insulted and my proposals were rejected. Not because they were wrong but the reality was I always doubted myself and was not able to fight for myself whatsoever.

Your true desires could not be hidden how hard you try. Love for Indian classical dance started blooming in me. I started getting attracted to dance shows and events. In the absence of my parents, I imitated the dancers on TV Shows. I always dreamt that I would perform someday on the stage in any of my annual school shows but that desires dampened when the routine performers filled the slot.

I gave up but my desires couldn't!

My mother noticed that my passion for dance was growing day by day. Indirectly she probed me with few questions and as result, she realised that I refrained myself from performing on stage, because of which, I would never be able to gather my confidence... ever. She tried talking to me but I declined. I never liked discussing those things which made me realize that I was weak. Because I knew I was!

We never like to discuss our flaws with anyone. And that is the reason we dislike our critic. However, if we take our critic as a normal unbiased person, we will find him better than a doctor. He is fine with our hatred, but not afraid to tell the truth. I was my biggest critic, but I disliked her the most!

Mom always caught in front of the TV shows where I aped dance steps. Indian classical dance was my favorite. But whenever I came to know that she was watching me, made me conscious. After secretly watching me perform numerous times she approached and appreciated me. She made me accept that I was a good performer. She realised that all she needs to do is to build up my confidence.

Appreciations are very beautiful, but my mother's words were not so influential to me when the case was regarding school performances. Among all my classmates I was the *dumbest*. Though this word is too strong to use I couldn't find a better adjective.

During the season of occasions and events when auditions for dancers took place, I had to fight and choose between my desires and personality. In the end, my personality would win... always!

Fighting with your weakness requires a lot of courage and while you are in that process a single downfall can shatter you.

This happened to me!

Since I was uplifted by my mother's appreciation, I gathered the confidence and was determined enough to reach out to my teachers and express my desires to perform in the annual dance show. It was no less than a battle for me. I had to prepare myself for everything.

Talking to someone was another hurdle for me. So before approaching her, I prepared a grammatically correct script so that I am not insulted in front of other students for wrong sentence framing. (Convent

Schools are very particular about English Communication).

"Ma'am I also wanted to perform with the dance troupe for the annual day event."

My sentence blew the minds of those girls who were the routine performers. The slots were already filled for the routine performers and there was no vacancy for anyone else. At least not for me!

My teacher gave me a cunning look and asked, "...do you take any dance training?"

"No, Ma'am!", I replied.

"Have you ever performed?" She asked again.

"No, Ma'am. But I can learn", I replied nervously.

I was shivering while I was talking to her. My hands and feet were all cold and for a speck of moment, I accused myself of taking this step.

"You cannot perform as you are not trained. Still, show us your dance moves", said my teacher as she wanted to reward me for my guts. Well that was the time when I had to prove myself.

A song was played for few minutes and I started performing. First few steps were swift and neat but then my glance fell upon the routine performers. They were giggling at me as if they were discussing what a terrible dancer I was. My confidence scale dropped to zero. Those glances made me so conscious that my focus was gone and my brain was confused. I ended up by messing things up. As a result, I was rejected and as a complimentary present I was tagged with the badge of 'absolutely pathetic dancer'.

I went back to my seat while the whole class was staring at me. Even the students who were non dancers tried to give me a pity look saying, "At least we know that we cannot dance!"

That day I learned that if we make a certain perception of something or someone, we will always take a decision according to that. The moment I told my teacher that I don't take dance training, at that very moment she made a conclusion out of it that I am a bad dancer and decided to reject me. Well, a perception cannot be changed if a person doesn't want to.

You are bullied when you are dumb but existing. I never existed except for 'Roll Number 44'. My classmates never bullied me as I was nonexisting. Expressing was a challenge for me! And when I expressed, I was either neglected or belittled. My shattering confidence was a concern to none but the one who was always observing me and that was my mother. She realised that if this will continue, apart from being a highly educated lady, I will turn taciturn.

So she decided to help me because she knew something was going on with me.

'*Incredible Dancer, Season four*' was then one of the trending reality shows for dancers. She decided that I should participate in the same. Without a second thought, she started the training. I never thought that I will ever be able to perform on a renowned platform when I was not even allowed to perform in the school events. My mom made it happen.

For any kind of Art, you need to bear deep love for it, not necessarily training. Training is for making things perfect and before perfection, you need to build a strong foundation.

A pot is created strong enough to bear the heat and drilling forces so as to carve any design or scripture on it's surface.

This was what she explained to me when I told her about the dance training incident that took place in my class. And when I was scared to lose she said,

Performance is bigger than Achievement!

Winning or Losing is just a relative terminology as the comparison is done with your competitors who participated, and that measuring scale for choosing the 'best' is in itself not very accurate.

You competition is with YOU. It totally depends on you whether you consider yourself a winner or a loser after your 'performance'!

These were not my words, these were her's and I believed the same! Getting a platform for the first time in my life was indeed an achievement for a person like me who was craving to perform on the annual days.

The Day of Event

During dance practices, I realised that my mother was a great dancer. Not only she taught me how to make swift movements, but she also took care of the apparel that I was going to put on the event.

Although my father never appreciated much of Dance and Music however after noticing my shattering confidence he gave permission to perform.

After rigorous practice, that day came along but also with the high fever. Due to my ill health, there were two options put forth me. To dance or to quit.

As parents, they suggested me not to, but how could I miss the first opportunity I waited for years. So I did what was meant to be done. I was the candidate number TL021.

In spite of high fever, I could feel the strange chill in my body. I felt numb. But that was the moment I had to turn my desires into memories worth remembering.

With shivering legs, I stepped on the dance floor. I found the Chief Guest sitting right in front of me. That day, I came to know what it feels when the whole world is staring at you.

While my soul was ready to perform, my body refrained from doing so. Teary eyes and terrible itching in my throat was distracting me as a result, I forgot all my dance steps. The cold temperature of the hall made me shiver.

Well, I had no option to stop or quit so I did what I was supposed to do. I started performing. When the song stopped, I felt so relaxed that I fell on my knees expressing my gratitude to all who were continuously watching and bearing me.

Among all in the crowd, I could see my parents clapping continuously! I did my best and that's what I wanted. What was the best according to the panel of judges, I never cared.

My mother grabbed me in her arms and hugged me tightly. At that particular moment, I felt I won! On the other hand, my father patted on my shoulders smiling, and said "Good Job Darling!". Well, that was another badge of pride for me.

My mother is very pragmatic. She observed the level of competition and realised that whatsoever the result would be, I will not be shortlisted in the winning list. As other candidates were well trained and came along with their dance Gurus. From their costumes to dance steps, everything was unquestionable. While on the other hand, my costume was made from traditional saree which was borrowed from some friend.

"We will have some snacks and then we will leave", said my mother.

"No, we shall wait for the result", exclaimed my dad. My father was less realistic but always very optimistic about my life. This time, he ruined her plot.

My mother gave a furious look to my dad while he was adamant to stay there. As a result, a heated 'Aadir – Ira' discussion took place. My mother tried to explain that her intention for me to was to give me a chance to participate in this competition so as to boost up my confidence which could again drown after hearing the result.

At last, my father had to give up as he couldn't agree more and took us to the stall nearby. Somewhere deeper in my heart I wanted to wait for the results but agreeing to the fact that I will definitely not win, I withdrew to express what I felt (the only thing that I was good at!).

My mother disrobed the sari and asked me to put on the frock that I brought along with me. I did the same making sure not to touch my makeup. I was looking beautiful for the first time in my life. The glossy lips with a tint of pink blush and neatly drawn liner highlighted my features so sharply that I realised I was also pretty. I kept on staring at the mirror. Yeah, I was beautiful! I never observed myself so keenly.

"Are you done, Sarah?" Asked my mother from behind the doors of the green room. I hurried and came out after putting on my casuals. I was feeling good. I started caring less about the result.

We went to the snacks stall nearby. While my father was about to take the change currency from the shop vendor for three loaded cheeseburgers **"Sarah Solanki"** loudspeaker blared. We were so clueless that we started moving towards the auditorium without burgers. We looked each other with doubt when the announcement was made for the second time and again my name was announced. All my mother could say was "Run and Grab it!".

I was far from the main stage, all I could do was to run with all my might to reach the stage. I was breathless when I heard, "Sarah Solanki, the winner in the category of Indian Classical Dance is cordially invited to receive her award from the veteran actor Mr. Irfan Khan!" said the host. My legs were shivering and my eyes were teary, I was still breathing heavily and my skin was all pale and hot because of fever. I am sure I might have been appearing funny with the blue frock and full on makeup but realizing that moment and holding the golden trophy while the audience clapping was the world for me.

"It's very easy to learn steps and perform, but feeling the art and performing is another level of understanding any art. Only true artist can do so and hence there is a difference between an Artist and a Performer. Sarah was really good at justifying the dance and she actually did what an Artist is supposed to do and hence we are honoring her with the first position." said the Chief Guest Irfan Khan.

Yes that was true! I performed as if it was my last performance. Yes, I forgot all the dance steps but put my heart and soul in each step and beat of the music. I was unsure what the total performance came out to be. Well, this was more than words for me. I never knew who I was. All I could see was my parents' gleaming faces and that made me happier. When I reached home, there were endless calls from relatives congratulating me and my parents. That was a moment of pride for me.

I realised that to prove your talent we need a trophy of success. If you lose in any competition you are definitely not talented. That will what the world will perceive. Well, that was not the reality. People think in a funny way and there is no doubt in that.

I was the winner and hence I was extremely talented. That was what I was told by the world.

I was in cloud nine and then I decided to announce my victory in my school, standing in front of the same teachers and students, face to face, who believed that I was a terrible performer.

"Mom, should I announce my achievement in my school?", I asked mom.

"Of course, you should", she exclaimed.

I was never waiting for this moment as I never expected that it will ever happen. But it did!

After the event my mother called me and explained the value of that trophy!

"Don't be so harsh on yourself. World we see you the way you portray yourself to them. This is just one trophy, there are more to come! Just believe yourself neither people nor environment!

Frame your life according to your choices not by others!

If you will not make choices, random things will choose you."

The next Monday morning was going to be exciting for me. After packing my backpack according to the schedule, I made ample space for that shiny trophy, which was trying to peep out even when I tightly chained my backpack. When I reached school, I was already smiling.

My friends noticed that and exclaimed, "What is in there?"

When I told them the story of my victory, they congratulated me. As expected, many were shocked and were unable to believe .

Even before announcing the incident to my classmates, I came to know that they already knew each and every detail of the event. Well, I thought I became popular, however, things that appear obvious might be a delusion in reality.

After the announcement and showcasing my gleaming reward to the whole school I entered my classroom. I could see the faces of my classmates and it appeared as if they were mocking at me. Later, I came to know about the rumor that was floating in the whole class. 'The competition was fixed by Sarah's parents. All were her relatives! She won out of favor and not by talent'.

This shattered me!

And it turned worse when a classmate exclaimed …"that's why we thought, how could she win when Ishita was already the participant of the show!"

That day I realised, people can do anything to satisfy their ego! ANYTHING!

Ishita was a routine performer and my classmate. She had been learning Bharatanatyam and Kathak since long. I never came to know that she was one of the participants in the competition. She was not able to handle the failure and hence framed this story. Well, I will not blame her as I had never tasted success till then.

Like any other child, I told everything to my mother. Her only statement was, "Just Ignore! We can never please the world by our achievements. They can only be pleased if they find some benefit in that."

I tried hard to understand what she explained me but I choose the wrong path again and as a result I started losing the courage to stand up and fight. The inferiority complex that was building in me was strengthening at each level of my life along with the illness, which I never discussed with my parents.

Chapter 7

The Reality of my Dreams

I often get defeated in battles ...but always win the wars!

Criticism was highly discouraged in my family. Be it for anyone. I have never seen my parents criticizing anyone and this habit was inculcated in me from the very beginning. Whenever I even tried to criticize people all my father used to say was, "first look at yourself, before pointing to anyone". Well, that was enough to keep a shut on my shutter.

Moral values are the identity of your family. But many times those moral values hinder your true virtue and vision. I never saw my grandparents however I was fortunate to live a few years of my life with my maternal grandparents. My maternal family was very decent and it was pretty obvious in my mother's personality.

Well, this is the most popular practice in every family. I cannot deny that, however, I cannot accept it cent percent also.

The biggest fallacy is "Elders are always Correct"

There is a word called 'Generation Gap' due to which there might be reasons that the elders are correct in a particular perception, though or idea but not always. I was facing indecisiveness while choosing between the correct or moral values, most of the time they coincide but sometimes they didn't. Out of 'respect' I started to hide things from my parents assuming I was wrong. I started to stay away from them.

I totally respect our culture and values but then our decision is what matters the most. I was not able to cross my parents and guardians as I doubted myself, or maybe self-doubt was thrust on me. For instance, education was considered as the highest priority and nothing less was accepted apart from that. The ideal career path means, good education, reputed job, and a good income. Well that was what the consummate and most secure path was. Any person who tried to think out of the way would either be considered immature and crazy or disrespectful towards the family.

If you are an Indian reader then you can relate to the above-mentioned statement very well.

My parents were very understanding but then they thought that they knew me very well. I felt that my parents started thrusting their ideas and perceptions on me than listening and understanding what I wanted and perceived the world to be.

Maybe I was too mute to be heard.

Maybe I never tried to express what I felt.

I choose to be the same!

My path was different although I realised this later by the change in my behavioral pattern and varied thought process. As my parents were best friends since college and we lived in a nuclear family. I had no one to share my thoughts to. I never tried to explain to my parents what I felt and what I have started believing and assuming in my own little world.

If you have educated parents then it's great, but if you have highly qualified degree holding parents, things are tougher as the world expects similar things from you or even more than that.

'You are the child of Professors. Subjects like Science and Mathematics are in your genes by default'. I was fed up with this statement which was very obvious from every visitor or relative.

I remember when I was in the fifth standard it all started. Friends circle of my parents comprised of most people who were Professors, Lecturers or Teachers by profession. All they could talk to me were about the equations of coordinate geometry and Newton's laws. They always intended to measure my knowledge and if I failed, they had an opportunity to give lectures on the importance of career and life.

Being the daughter of highly intellectual people was a challenge for me as for the society I had to prove the power of my genes constantly. The person I hated the most was Mr. Rajat who was my father's co-worker.

It was another common day when I found him in my living room munching snacks.

"Hello Sarah darling, how are you?"

To his statements, I would always smile and nodded. So that day was no different.

The next few minutes of discussion were about studies and the best subjects to make your career in. Honestly, I was not interested however I could not argue. So I had to grab a pen and paper and answer what he wanted me to.

He gave me two questions on directions and three on Algebra. Algebra was easy to solve but when I had to solve geometry, I got stuck. I was not supposed to ask as I avoided listening to his lecture again while my father sat mute and helpless. So I waited for him to leave.

Ninety minutes passed but he was still sipping his tea. I knew his intention.

Well, these incidents were very common in my life. I was supposed to be the 'brilliant' one. And for that, I had to prove myself to my relatives every time, be it a festival, event or just any other common day.

That was very frustrating and demotivating!

I was judged by the marks I scored, the way I behaved etc. I disliked humans as they had a habit of assuming and bringing a conclusion out of anything and everything.

A person is brought to trial and suffers from pre-assumed attributes which if not matched then, you are a fail. This was what the world believed.

I tried to understand people, but I failed.

I started keeping myself away from all those people who measured or tried to measure my caliber every now and then and brought me to test. Like always my mother had been observing these things since long.

She was always doubtful of the personality I was turning into.

It was said that I never had good friends and I never put efforts to make any. I had my own world where I lived in fantasy. I used to talk to myself and stay happy. I started to stay away from Piya, Mani or any other friend. I knew how to be happy in my own world of imagination. My imaginary friends never tried to thrust their views or decisions on me. I was the ruler of my own dynasty. But for the real world, I was developing a disease.

I could recall many incidents when I had my imaginary friends along with me. At times there were moments when my parents had to leave home in emergency. At that moment I had two friends with whom I interacted. We played together and they listened to me patiently, whatever I had to say or explain. They believed whatever I said.

My parents spotted me talking to myself. I could hear voices in my head and to that I started responding. My extreme sensitivity and imaginations were becoming an issue for me. As for the real world that was not considered natural, my parents tried to counsel me but in vain.

Like any other parents, my parents also had expectations from me. Especially my father. They had their dreams unfulfilled because they got married and responsibilities fell upon them. Being a patriotic person my father wanted me to join any of the Defense or Civil Services. The difficult part was the training. So every morning he made sure that I woke up while we together go for a practice. I disliked that.

As it's aptly said that if you don't choose an option for yourself, someone else will thrust their options on you.

This was what exactly happened. I cannot blame my father for this as I had no knowledge of my career path so my dreams were through my father which was also shattered when I was diagnosed with weak vision.

My vision was deteriorating and I was not able to understand the reason behind it. In spite of healthy food and good lifestyle I was not fine with the visibility strength, I was having at that time.

I was in standard seventh and (I could recall that very well) wherever I was seated in class, the content written on the blackboard was never visible to me. The issue turned grave and I had to tell my parents as there was no escape for it.

Even today in their late fifties my parents never required glasses so it was impossible for me to make them believe that I had weak eyesight. When diagnosed, the doctor remarked that my both eye vision was equally very weak and that was -2.75 (myopia) which was too low for the first stage and at that tender age.

And this was how specs became my forever companions.

The question was why suddenly my eye vision dropped when my diet was healthy, genes were strong and there was no indication of weak vision in my bloodline.

Later, my father had to accept that Defense Services were not for me so now I should try for Civil Services i.e IAS examination.

IAS is the dream of many. It stands for Indian Administrative Services. Rigorous hard work and devotion with some luck were required to clear the exams. In India, more than sixty percent of students have attempted IAS at least once in their lifetime. Few had the same dream however their dreams are either shattered by tough selection process or by reservation system prevalent in our country. I found out that my father's dream was gradually becoming my dream.

Knowing that marks could be the biggest issue in my life I started studying really hard. Physics, Chemistry, Geography, and History all were good but when it came to memorizing routes or solving problems related to directions like geometry or logical/analytical questions related to directions, I was always stuck. My brain never understood the difference between right or left or any standard directions (North, South, East, West). Even today if someone instantly ask me where do the sunrise from, I might remember the terminology, but if you ask me to point the direction of the east, I will not be able to do so.

For twelve years I went to the same school, however, I was not able to remember the directions i.e where to turn left or right. This case is true, even today. In scientific terms, it is called Topological Disorientation. I was not aware of the terminology back then but this was not a good sign for a lifetime. I realised much later why I was always lost when I rode my bicycle. Dots were connecting and time was giving me answers on each step.

After proper introspection, I realised why I couldn't understand the problems which had direction related queries. Similarly, I was not able to understand and register the routes of places where I visited frequently. Many people tried to counsel me and provided me many strategies to learn routes but I was not able to do so even after trying with all my might.

Not only this I was unable to decide the difference between my hands. During physical training sessions or sports periods when I was asked to raise my right hand, I was always confused. Since I had to act in the spur of that moment, I often raised the wrong hand. I can remember how I ruined many sports functions and dance movement which demanded coordination. I got answers to many questions and the answer was **Topological Disorientation.**

I was ashamed to share this weakness with anyone, so I had to find the solution for that, all by myself.

Nature always helped me in one way or the other. There was a mole in my right-hand. So whenever anyone asked to put forth the right hand, I checked the mole and confidently responded. This was a secret engraved in my heart.

I started observing my weaknesses which was developing over time. One of the few were, tying shoelace or untying that. I was always stuck in those threads. Howsoever I tried, I got stuck. Another one was remembering dance steps or any physical activity which required defined movement on a particular beat. Things may sound silly but not remembering basic things that are integral in day to day life costed me much!

Days went by and I tried my best not to discuss these issues with my parents. My illness and growing sensitivity towards nature was making my life tough. I tried my best to hide my weaknesses but somewhere I knew it couldn't be hidden from my parents whatsoever.

There was a room at my home where I never entered. I was not able to understand the reason behind it. It was a small room which was extended inward to utilize the space. It was well constructed. The size of the room was not very large but it had a strange aura that made me uncomfortable. I never understood the reason behind that. I would not say it was possessed but the vibes were not good whenever I tried entering the room. I avoided using that room.

I tried to explain this to my parents but like always they thought I was making things up. Not only my parents but if anyone would have overheard my conversations with my parents, would have called me crazy. I had no one to discuss what I felt except my imaginary friends. I would never blame my parents for this as they were a part of the real world and these absurd things sounded stupid to them, which was absolutely normal!

I wanted someone to step in my shoes and understand what I actually felt as I was not able to understand and clearly express to my parents, what was going on with me.

According to Human Psychology: You can understand the other person better only if you have the same guilt or problem with you or else it will be just some random theory for you.

Same happened to me. I expected my parents to understand me, which was useless!

I had to burst out but I had no one to share my thoughts to (and my imaginary friends never responded to my queries). Helplessly, I started maintaining a diary. It was a large Tagebuch with glossy emerald cover. I named it, *'My Emerald Diary'*. I used to write almost everything I felt, observed and experienced. Directly or indirectly they all were related to my pain and sufferings.

"You are just overthinking!"

I was used to this statement from my parents. It was getting difficult for me to give an explanation of how helpless I felt. I was a patient and my only doctors were my parents. I believed them.

Mom and Dad had a strange way of dealing with things. If they had any problem which could be solved right away they will sort it on that speck of moment. If the same problem could not be solved at that moment they will never let that problem interfere their lives. They will shift their thoughts and efforts to something better and productive. But what if that problem is not situational but an indication of disease?

'The more you ponder over a thought or idea, it will register deeper into your mind'

Ignoring your problems and moving ahead so that it cannot interfere you to do something better is an Art.

I wanted to learn that art from my parents. So, I decided to fight with what was getting wrong with me.

I decided to learn routes and directions!

I took a big chart paper and marked North, South, East and West directions, to understand better. I placed that chart paper right in front of my study table. After about a week I felt that I had done my homework and it was time to implement my knowledge.

The other day I took permission from my parents to go on a ride so as to understand better what I memorised. My mother was more than pleased to know that I was willing to go all by myself as (I thought) she came to know that I had difficulty in remembering routes.

It was six in the evening when I took my scooty and drove towards my school. The distance of my school from my home was hardly 3-4 km. I was confident that I will be able to accomplish what I have been trying since long however to my misfortune I couldn't. On the first right turn of the route I was lost which was beyond my expectations. I strained my brain but I couldn't recall where to go next. I had to call dad for help.

This was not the end of trying. I tried many times, but I couldn't memorize routes. My brain was unable to process spatial information due to which I could not map or track routes. After infinite attempts, I gave up!

I started staying alone. I had no wishes, no choices, no greed like any other child. In short, I loved to be alone with all my expressions and emotions trapped in *My Emerald Diary*. It was turning very difficult for my parents to mold and bring me to the right track.

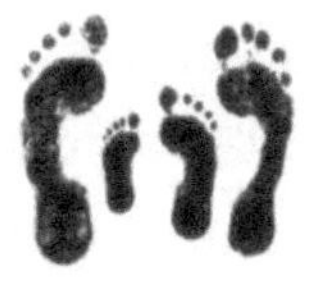

Chapter 8

The Peak

Ocean is the only place on earth where we can simultaneously feel power and loneliness.

Topological Disorientation was not the only case with me. At the age of fifteen, I start experiencing some absurd incidents in my life. My parents have observed me blabbering multiple times while I was sleeping. I was always hyperactive when I was meant to be unconscious. Although I used my right hand to write, I was a lefty from birth. My pre-nursery teacher forcefully trained me write with the right hands, however, I was told that I started writing with the left hand. Today I am equally comfortable writing with both hands though speed may vary. The left side of my limbs were always more active and highly sensitive than the right one.

Once when I was returning from my school, I felt acute pain on the left side of my body. I thought it could be because of stress or the heavy backpack that I often carried along to school. For a few days I kept mum but then I had to tell this to my mother as it was turning chronic and unbearable. My parents assumed that I was facing some stress in my studies or maybe I was undergoing some hormonal changes in my body. Maybe that could be true. Like always, I believed them.

As the days passed by the intensity of the pain increased. Day by day it was becoming unbearable for me to live in that pain. I was becoming short-tempered as the pain was testing my patience. My mind turned fidget and irresistible. Loud noise, strong smell and bright light started hurting me. My body was becoming vulnerable which was reflected on my skin at night. Red itchy patches all over the body, which gradually disappeared in daylight.

Even in the most silent hour, a pin drop sound could impede my peace. My actions and reactions were becoming visible to the world as I could not hide that anymore.

One of my relatives visited my parents few months later and showed his eager to meet me. I hated visitors as they always tried to judge my knowledge. But this person was different.

He was an elderly man with bright eyes and light scars on his face. The wrinkles on his forehead were so neatly drawn that his face would have appeared incomplete without those fine lines. He was wearing a pair of gold-rimmed glasses. To me, he appeared angelic or maybe it was just a random conclusion drawn by my perception.

According to the family tree he was my grandfather as he was the cousin brother of my grandfather. In the first glance of mine, he might have concluded that something was bothering me and making me unhappy. He tried to ask me a few questions and tried to read between the lines, whenever I answered. He might have realised that those questions were upsetting me, so he changed into a friendly tone, casually asking, "What you like to do in your free time Sarah?" His voice was heavy yet attractive.

"I love to write.!", I replied although the correct answer was very different from this one and it would have been like, "I am always engrossed with my mind and struggling with random thoughts, emerging from there"

He smiled at me with the answer and asked me if I would allow him to read few of my creations.

That was the first time when someone asked to read my creations. I was more than happy. I brought my Emerald Diary and handed over to him. I expected him to smile but he appeared worried after reading first few pages. My father was sitting beside me and my mother just entered the room holding a tray with four mugs of coffee.

"I kept fighting throughout... for Life!

But Death took away the trophy!

...I am not scared of him..,

I just want him to take me away... silently

...for I know he would never share me with anyone!"

And all he could say was, "Why do you choose to write on these negative topics, you are too young to understand the meaning of death, dear."

My father never tried to read or interfere in what I wrote or believed in but he never expected this coming up, while the elderly man was continuously staring at me as if he was trying to search some answers. His wrinkles stretched and appeared deeper and darker. Suddenly I burst out in tears and ran away from the place. He came to me and asked me if I was fine. I tried to control myself as I was not able to understand how to explain to him what I was going through.

He tried to take me back in the same discussion but I denied. He interacted with my father and asked him if he could show him the house so that he had an opportunity to talk to him alone. I never understood what was going on however when he entered the room which I disliked, he appeared as upset as I would have been while entering the room. He remarked that there was something wrong with that room and even I felt the same but I was not able to give words to what I actually felt there.

Then after pondering for fifteen to twenty minutes, he said that the architecture of that room was not fine and placement of the mirror was also very wrong. I cannot assure whether he was accurate but he had the same absurd feeling while entering the room. I was happy to know that this time I was not wrong and my instincts were correct.

Before bidding him goodbye, he told something to my father after which dad's outlook towards me immediately changed. He tried to read my diary and got shocked and embarrassed. Then he strictly ordered that I was not allowed to continue the practice of diary writing ever again unless I write something good and happy. Although he was trying to help me however I was extremely offended by his act.

Diary was gone but my sickness and sensitivity was still prevalent. This continued till the next three years after which another problem started.

I had a cousin who was very close to me. We had the age difference of more than ten years. He pampered me more than my parents. He was not only my big brother but my best friend too. Although my aunt's family was about fifty miles away from our home, he used to travel often just to meet me. He was no less than a real brother for me.

One unfortunate day we came to know that he met with an accident and died on spot. It was a traumatic incident for all of us. I was about ten when I realised what was death.

He was very close to my heart and after his death I often suffered from hallucination of his voices and images of his faces. His face was not deformed but he had no hairs on his scalp!

After this incident, I recalled a very similar incident that occurred when Sister Christina died few years ago. A dream with a figure of Nun without any hairs on the scalp and the other day, news of Sister Christina's demise!

I was extremely disturbed!

We spend most of the time with ourselves but the problem is we never listen to our internal voices but others. Somewhere deep inside we all feel 'what if I am wrong?' This thought brings us to trial many times, as a result, we

I was going with the flow and never stopping to introspect myself. Neither was I explaining things to my parents, nor allowing them to enter my life.

A few years later my aunt was diagnosed with uterus cancer and the treatment was going well but suddenly, one midnight of the second month of the year, I saw the flashes of her face. I was alarmed when I saw her bald in my dream, and that made me jolt out of the sleep in the midnight, sweating. I had to tell this to my father so I did. I shared him my past experiences too.

At this, my father scolded me and said that I have gone crazy as that could not possibly happen because her chemotherapy was successful and she was out of danger as claimed by doctors. I was clueless and went back to my bedroom. I was not able to understand what was happening to me. Believe me, nothing can be worse than foreseeing the death of people you know and have spent significant time with.

One gloomy day of March a careless mistake of doctor costed her life. I was numb, so was my father. I started hating myself. I could not control and bear the flashes which predicted people's death. I told everything to my parents as they also started believing what I saw and felt. I was not happy and life like this was soaking my soul.

This was not the first incident, it was fifth or sixth time when I predicted someone's death. My high sensitivity was becoming the reason for extreme disorganized thoughts and ideas. I tried to explain everything to my parents but their method of treating any grave situation was either to divert your mind from that or to forget.

It was not easy for me to forget or divert. It was becoming a part of my daily routine. I saw the images of all the dead people or people who were about to die and I knew them. It was uncontrollable and suffocating. I was helpless and wanted to get out of it.

Similar incidents kept meddling me and I was not able to understand what was going on. At the age of seventeen, I clearly realised, that I can foresee deaths of some people. This was getting out of control and I started losing my consciousness.

Where the girls of my age were tasting life, I was fighting with the complexity of my dreams.

After visiting numerous doctors like Neurologists, Psychiatrists, Dermatologists, and even Ophthalmologists. No trace was found. The Neurologist claimed that I was having some symptoms of spondylitis because of the chronic pain in my back body and with the prescription, I was offered to wear that cervical neckband which was awful. The Dermatologists restricted me from eating fried and spicy food. The Ophthalmologists had no clue of what was wrong with me. And the Psychiatrist said that I was facing some bad relationship with my family due to which I was having a symptom of acute anxiety. Well, I couldn't say that he was totally wrong because it was true that I was not able to explain many things to my family.

Among all these doctors, the Psychiatrist was able to get hold of strong emotional fluctuations and the only advice he gave to my parents were, that I should be taken extra care of. He was not able to catch the exact symptom of my disease but he realised that it was not something natural and could not be treated by traditional medication process. Different medicines, regular X-rays, CT scans etc were all in vain. They showed no symptoms of deformity.

Hearing voices of strangers, seeing faces of known people who were dead or are about to die, growing sensitivity towards sound, smell or bright light was giving me every reason to end my life. As I knew I could not bear or ignore all these things for a lifetime. Each passing day, the effect was growing and I was helpless. Next stage of my disease was *Intermittent explosive disorder*.

It was a pity state of mine.

I was the reason to start and I was the only one who could end it all.

When I was in standard twelfth with board exams about to approach all my classmates were busy preparing while I was struggling with myself. Like always, my relatives already started the auction process for my board exam marks while I was not over with my hallucinations and precognitive dreams.

My parents saved me by not expressing my illness to anyone. They tried to deal it in their own way. My father started visiting different doctors for their help and suggestions while my mother started taking extra care of my health. On the other hand, my little sister was the one who patiently listened to all my gibberish talks.

(Yes! Aadir and Ira were blessed with another girl child who was about seven years younger to Sarah. Fortunately, she didn't showed the symptoms of any abnormality like Sarah.)

It was high time when I realised, that my disease was turning into an omen for me and my family.

I tried committing suicide by engulfing handful of paracetamol tablets!

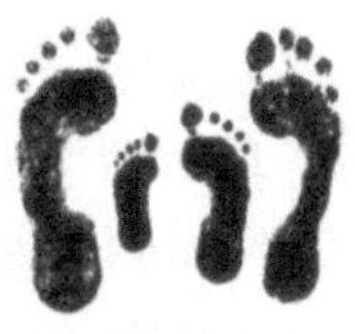

Chapter 9

Schizophrenia and Precognition

Correct or Incorrect, Good or Bad, Sin or Bliss, Best or Worst are all relative terms!

The day we understand that... we understand life.

Schizophrenia

Source: Mental Health Nursing, Verna Benner Carson

Individuals with schizophrenia experience hallucinations (most reported are hearing voices), delusions (often bizarre or persecutory in nature), and disorganized thinking and speech. Social withdrawal, sloppiness of dress and hygiene, and loss of motivation and judgment are all common in schizophrenia.

*Distortions of self-experience such as feeling as if one's thoughts or feelings are not really one's own to believing thoughts are being inserted into one's mind, sometimes termed **passivity phenomena**, are also common. There is* *often an observable pattern of emotional difficulty, for example, lack of responsiveness. Impairment in social cognition is associated with schizophrenia as are symptoms of paranoia. Social isolation commonly occurs. Difficulties in working and long-term memory, attention, executive functioning, and speed of processing also commonly occur. In one uncommon subtype, the person may be largely mute, remain motionless in bizarre postures, or exhibit purposeless agitation, all signs of* **catatonia***. People with schizophrenia often find facial emotion perception to be difficult. It is unclear if the phenomenon "called thought to block", where a talking person suddenly becomes silent for a few seconds to minutes, occurs in schizophrenia.*

About 30 to 50 percent of people with schizophrenia fail to accept that they have an illness or comply with their recommended treatment. Treatment may have some effect on insight.

Precognitive Dreams

Source - Patrick McNamara Ph.D, Psychology Today

Precognitive dreams are dreams that appear to predict the future through a sixth sense.

Quantum effects in physics have been used by new agers and others to argue for all kinds of silly things concerning

I woke up in the hospital and like always, my family was near me.

Their strange silence was asking many questions from me. My father's eyes were swollen and appeared as if he has cried. My mother was great at pretending but I could see that she was also not happy with the step I took. After a few hours later my father came near me, grabbed the steel stool and sat by my iron bed.

All he said, that I could remember... even today.

"Life is not easy and you are not allowed to quit the game in the middle.

You are supposed to fight.

We understand what you are going through and we are in this together as a team.

Just because you own the disease that doesn't gives you the right to kill yourself."

After a pause, he continued,

"When you were born, I was told that you could not survive for more than five years but I believed that you will.

You were not able to breath when you just entered the world.

But today you are seventeen and fine.

I could have let you go, but I was stubborn and you should be too."

He kept staring me with his eyes full of tears.

"It's easy to die, but very difficult to live.

Show me your strength by living and not dying.

I know what you are facing is not easy to bear for anyone but learn to fight than to quit.

It may appear that you are alone and fighting all by yourself, which is absolutely wrong.

We all are standing beside you.

I was under strong medication and was not able to exactly remember his words but whatsoever I understood, sounded sensible to me.

I tried killing myself out of helplessness, as no one was able to help me. But after that incident, even a thought of giving up, scared me. Yeah, it was either the guilt after taking the step or maybe I wanted to live!

I started studying more about my disease and tried to understand what was going wrong with me because the only answer could be gained by gaining knowledge about the topic. I started searching for answers everywhere because I had no options but to live for the people who loved me.

Each passing night when the red patches appeared after the sunset, my craving for answers drastically increased. It was late but I realised that I cannot ask my parents for any more help and have to move on.

As life moved on I had to keep moving along with it. Sometimes, it appeared like a treadmill where I had to match with the pace and speed accordingly or else I would slip off the track. Bearing the pain at every moment I had the only option to keep up the pace as I was not strong enough to kill myself again.

A Love Story that Never Existed

We humans are vulnerable and the weakest when we desire for love. This happens basically in three stages of life. Firstly, when we are teens and wish for a partner who understands us more than our family. Secondly, when we have faced a serious heartbreak and it is becoming really difficult for us to recover. At this stage, we are like a 'money' plant. From wherever we get the support we get inclined towards that! And the third kind of love is when we are mature and desire to live with someone who understands us.

Love or infatuation in teenage is very natural and full of fantasies. It brings all the colors of life. But what if it's just imaginary and not a real one?

Like any other teen, I was attracted to this guy named Karan.

It is psychologically proved that you often fall in love with the person who shows the beauty in you. I was in love with a guy from my coaching institute. It was not infatuation, it was an assumption. As I mentioned prior, I had two imaginary friends of which one was a girl and the other was a boy. The character of the imaginary boy matched with Karan and I thought that I was in love with him.

When he came to know about my feelings towards him, he tried to explain and express that he never felt the same however I was not ready to accept reality. For a very long period of time, he considered me his friend while I had different emotions towards him. He concluded from my absurd behavior, that whenever I will face reality, I will try to harm myself. It was a very sensitive issue for me. So he played around as he had no other option.

For a long time I 'thought' I was in a relationship however, I never was. Except for his name, I didn't knew anything about his family, likes or dislikes or his routine.

'Karan' for me was just a character I thought I loved, like two imaginary friends of mine.

Chapter 10

The Transition Phase

You don't create your passion... it's there since your existence or maybe it's the only reason of your existence.

I was clueless about my future. I had no plans as my mind was already keeping me busy with absurd thoughts and ideas. I had to move on. So like my other friends I decided to join a college and continue my education.

As my parents always believed in the 'distraction theory' they were very happy with this decision of mine and no doubt that was the best decision of life.

As I was moving along with time, my disease was going and growing along with me. I was becoming short tempered and rude because of regular irresistible flashes, dreams and never-ending red patches. I was helpless as even doctors were not able to understand what was wrong with me.

My parents felt that the only thing that could help me was 'moving on'. But that was not easy. I wanted them to understand me and listen to me and all they wanted was not to discuss the state and keep moving on by focusing on things that mattered.

I moved to a different city! It was a whole new experience.

It's a rule in my family that we never discussed or pondered on negative thoughts so, whenever I tried to discuss my illness to my parents on call they often changed the topic.

Depression is NOT a disease but a state of mind.

I felt so disowned that I wanted to seek the attention of many. Staying away from family and realising the truth behind my relationship with Karan, shattered me. The word 'Depression' was the best alternative word. If I would have ever tried to give proper explanation of my disease, people would have either not believed me or called me crazy. Intermittent Explosive Disorder is very rare in Migraine, but I had no other alternative to use.

Whenever I had these attacks, I covered up with terminologies like these. Somewhere, wanted a social life. Above all, I wanted the attention of people but I was scared of my reality and weaknesses.

No doubt I was closer to my dad, but we had clashes too. I wanted him to understand me while he wanted me to get distracted from my state of mind and focus on the other experiences of life. It was his way of treating my illness.

Although I was undergoing antipsychotic medication, these were few counseling tips that were told to my father and he was following that. The problem was, I wanted to be listened and that too without interruption!

Like any other day, that day too I had a fight with dad and I was trying to stay away from my hostel mates so as to not let them know what kind of father-daughter relationship we had. While I was strolling in the terrace and talking to my dad, my glance fell upon a slim and tall girl who was strolling near stairs, staring at her mobile. She was a newcomer.

"One day when I will leave you all forever, then you will get to know my worth Papa...".

Whenever I tried to explain my state to him, he changed the topic and this agitated me the most. A simple conversation turned to high level of heated up argument. I was almost crying on phone and I was sure that she overheard me as I was very loud and clear. When I realised that, I got distracted and changed my direction.

While I was on call, she was following me, trying to listen to the conversation. I had to disconnect the call as I was getting conscious of her involvement.

"Hi…" I took the first breath after the call when I heard an overwhelming voice from behind.

"Hello", I felt absurd as she was being over friendly and I was just the contrast.

"So, have you made a plot of how you are going to die as I overheard your conversation with your Dad! You seem very eager to die…", she blurted.

At this, I felt offended as I was not expecting this statement from a stranger who has no idea of my life.

"I can offer you my balcony to commit suicide as I cannot see any balcony area in your room".

At this, I furiously said, "Madam, you don't know anything so please stop meddling in my affairs".

"Okay, I am just trying to help you… calm down buddy. Anyway, would you like to grab a cup of tea at my place… let's solve your problem!", I guess she realised by my facial expression that I was getting out control so she immediately changed the topic.

If I would have been a little stubborn and not taken that step towards her room, then I would have had one of the biggest banes of my life.

I took that step and from there, things started to become easier for me.

Natasha was her name.

Although the architectural design of each hostel room was exactly the same, the placement of furniture made each room look different.

Natasha's room was large with a balcony attached to it.

As I entered I saw an endearing face of girl with curly hairs who was sitting on her bed, doing her assignments. I guessed she was her roomie.

We exchanged glances along with a formal smile when Natasha offered me some freshly prepared tea. There were a strange comfort and positive aura around this girl and I adored that.

You are attracted to only those characteristics in people which you want to possess. Well, the same thing happens if you are jealous of someone. The reality is you are never envious of one's success but you want to be successful as well. That inferiority complex in you might make you feel jealous of that person.

So if you dislike someone and cannot find the reason behind it then accept that you are jealous of that person and suffer from intense inferiority complex.

The only truth is, you want to be like that Person.

I was not jealous of Natasha, I adored the way she thought. Maybe I wanted to be like her.

"So this was the balcony I was talking about". She said pointing at a small extension of the room which was converted into a balcony.

"You can come and jump from here anytime you want to." She gave a sarcastic look while saying that. Well, that sounded stern and funny. I was speechless.

Over few sips of strong tea we shared our introductions. I loved the way she spoke. Her personality could easily stir energy in the dull and gloomy air. A perfect blend of confident mind and peaceful heart.

Everyone loves to be with someone whom they find comfort with and are not ashamed to be original. I realised at the very moment that I am not uncomfortable to share my reality with this girl. I found my best friend!

Natasha was a catalyst in my life in stirring my sorrows and giving me the energy to fight all odds. I had one more reason to live and fight.

In my college days also I remember few incidents where I was confused between dreams and reality. For example, my dreams were so real that I felt like *Deja Vu* moments. Every minute detail of the event, even the color of clothes that people were wearing were exact similar to what I saw in dreams. Scientifically it is also called *hallucinations*.

I tried to test this one day when in random dream I saw my friend Ryan standing on my left side and asking for something. His conversation was not very clear but I could recognize him very clearly wearing a gray T-Shirt with black patches on it.

Ryan was a classmate. We never went out on a trip together as he had a different friend circle than mine. In short, we never interacted unless there was some assignment or project related issues. That was the beginning of a session and I reported to the class very late. My eyes were searching for Ryan. I turned around to check if Ryan was present. Well, I was relaxed to know that he was not present that day. I tired to asked his friend and he confirmed that he was out of town and will not be able to attend classes before he returns from his hometown.

I took a deep breath in acceptance when in the next second I saw Ryan standing by my left side and asking me something. For few minutes I was numb! I was about to say "What the hell... how come you are here?"

"Sarah... are you fine?" Ryan exclaimed after watching my alarmed face.

"How come you are here...?" - I asked him in a hoarse voice.

"Why shouldn't I?" He enquired.

"But just a few minutes ago Jai told me that you were out of town!" - I asked taking a deep breath. I was shivering.

"Yeah, I had to be here today as I had to visit the CBSE office for my mark sheet. Since your cousin is in this field I wanted to ask for your help. Only you can help me." Ryan explained.

Ryan was wearing the exact gray colored T-Shirt with dark patches and was standing right beside me in the left direction, positioned in the same way as I saw a few hours ago.

It may appear scripted and as it is hard to believe and even harder to explain!

For a few minutes, I was just trying to accept what I saw. I tried to make every other possibility not to think or relate, but in vain.

This was just a common random event which I saw. I wanted answers of these flashes, dreams or hallucinations. I had sleepless nights and my brain was always weary and tired even after resting and sleeping for at least eight hours or more, everyday!

Case Study:

Whenever we want others to listen to us, there are very few who actually listen, 90 percent of people will either give their suggestions according to their experience or will relate their condition with yours and grief more than you. Only 10 percent of people (or maybe less) will listen to you. They may or may not have a solution to your problem but their patiently listening to you will serve the purpose of what you were looking for.

The brain never works on it's own, it works according to the instructions it's provided. Your fingers will not snap unless it is asked to snap. Even the smallest action that we think is involuntary, is not. It is the reflexes that act according to the surroundings and brain is asked to do so. So if the brain is told you are ill, it's the job of the brain to manage your body temperature and metabolism accordingly. My brain was told that he was ill!

Later, I realised that I was having the symptoms of **Schizophrenia**. I was diagnosed with the same.

Living with imaginary people, suffering from topological disorientation, and seeing and hearing things that never actually existed were few of the symptoms of schizophrenia. Since it's a field of wide study, this disease was not clearly defined because of varied symptoms. Even doctors are not able to clearly define this disease. Precognitive dreams were another part of it.

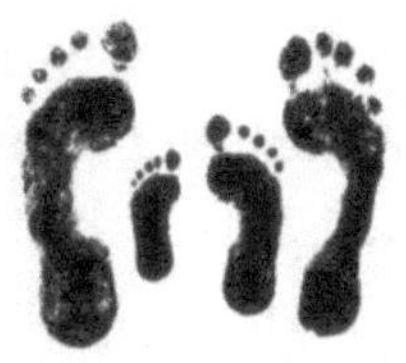

Chapter 11

A Step Ahead!

When people feel they have no control over what is happening, they tend to see non-existent patterns and unrelated pictures, and believe in conspiracy theories.

Getting placed in 'big organizations' has always a higher preference than what your job profile is. Of course, salary package matters but more important is the brand name. Infosys, TCS, Google were few of the names which raised the eyebrow of any person who heard of it first.

Like always, I had no desires and aspirations of mine.

I started giving interviews. Every time the HR asked me "Why you want to join the organization" my answer would be the standard one and never the real one. I started following the standard procedure of the crowd. Things were getting difficult for me! Very Difficult!

I got many job offers but I was never happy. In the span of two years, I changed four organizations. Not because the work was bad, but because I was not feeling good there. Mysore, Bangalore, Noida were few of the places I lived for work when I ultimately got an opportunity to work in Chennai.

Chennai was a sorted city with beautiful people, positive vibes and aura. Although I faced a lot of cultural differences there, I realised that even differences are good. We are just too clingy to our ways and methods. I was not happy with the work but I was very happy with the versatility of the city.

My disease was continuously bugging me but I kept ignoring, pretending to be stronger than before. I learned to ignore and move on. I spoke less about my disease and more about my future.

Things were going fine when the year 2015 showed it's evil shadow to the city. Flood attacked the whole city. Due to continuous rains for about seven days the whole city was floating in water. It was the dark era for the city. Stuck traffic, no bank services, no food supply... nothing. Due to frequent power cuts, we were not able to even charge the batteries of our mobile phones and it was getting difficult for us to connect to our family members.

The condition worsen when we were told to keep an identity proof with us all day long .This precaution was taken so as to identify the bodies in case they are drowned. That day I realised anything can happen the next moment.

I was residing in a hostel where almost ninety percent of girls were from nearby cities like Coimbatore and Pondicherry. They went early with their relatives. Even the hostel owner left us in this adversity. I was with few other North Indian girls who had nowhere to go. No food, no electricity, and no support.

We had to fight for our lives!

Since there was no electricity and continuous rains, we were not able to connect with anyone. The water level was rising every day. One of us noticed that few helicopters were tracing areas and were searching for people who were required to rescue from that adverse situation. We decided to go to the terrace to ask for help. Our situation was so bad that we tried our best to get ourselves out. On the other hand, our family members were equally worried. We all had one last wish and that was to see our family before we die. After trying to give signals for two-three days continuously, a scout spotted us.

We were asked to tie ropes on our waists while a commander was pulling us up. It was a strange feeling that they were helping us knowing that their life was in the same danger. A young boy was the pilot and the commander was in his late thirties. Since it was very early in the morning, my red patches were still visible and I was feeling the chronic pain on the left side of my body. I decided to ignore, grabbed my jacket and covered myself well.

We three climbed the helicopter and thanked the team. While I was adjusting myself on the cold iron bench, I saw that the commander who helped us, was already injured and was bleeding profusely. He asked for the first aid box from the pilot and did his own dressing. His nameplate was displaying the name 'Capt. Asad Malik'.

After a long silence, I couldn't resist asking, "How could you do all this?"

He was dressing the wound and this sudden question made him smile at me. He said, "I am not sure what you are asking about? But if you are asking why I saved you, then it was my duty and I love to do it."

"But who loves to risk their lives and do these things", I could not control my curiosity. To this he answered:

"Whatever you love to do can cost you and will cost you anything.

But unlike typical businessmen you will not think of profit or loss.

I may have many distractions but my passion drives me not my circumstances.

Tomorrow even if I die out of any reason, I will die in peace as every second which I lived, I lived for my dreams.

Our journey may end anytime and that it is out of our control. What is in our control is, how we performed on our journey."

He added,

"With true passion, courage is complimentary.

Don't get driven by people. Don't prove anything to them. Make them believe in you!"

His words were very powerful. I could see that even after dressing, his blood was trying to push through the bandage of his wound. He tried to stop that with his other hand by clasping across the wound. It appeared a little painful as he groaned for a second.

He looked into my eyes and realised that I was feeling pity for him because of the injury. To this he replied,

"Don't feel pity on my state. It's an insult for me.

A warrior is also a doctor of his wounds.

Only he can and will have the potential to heal his wounds.

He just has to believe that it will get cured gradually and everything will be fine.

You just need to trick your brain that you are perfectly healthy and it will believe you."

His words were engraved in my heart and soul!

We landed to army cantonment and were given shelter there. I still thank each and every element that helped us to get out of the flood. It was a miracle that saved our lives.

A few days later I came to know that Capt. Asad Malik passed away because of the deep wound and infection caused by that injury. Apart from being a courageous soldier, he was a painter too. It was his last wish to get his coffin painted with vibrant colors while he bids his final goodbye to the world! The troop followed his instructions.

What a man he was!

The dark era settled and we all were finally able to connect with our families. I boarded the first flight to my hometown. I was so exhausted with the circumstances that now all I wanted was to see my parents.

What goes along, comes along.

Our life is not like a novel with clearly defined chapters and events. Everything is connected with everything and incidents of pasts will reoccur.

These incidents affected me so much that I fell ill. For hours and days, I suffered from attacks where my body was almost paralyzed and the pain was unbearable.

Medically speaking it was the peak moment and I had to make the choice to live or to quit. The same symptoms were becoming more obvious. I was becoming out of control and my aggressiveness caused stress in my family. I was developing high sensitivity to light, smell or noise. I was on high dose of medication and my mind was forced to be unconscious as my body was already numb.

After numerous attempts the only statements of the doctors were:

"We cannot save her as she has lost the hope to live.

Medicines are just triggers which will lose power if she loses the will to recover."

I was losing the hope and so was my family except for my father. All he could say was, *"I cannot afford to lose her as she all that I dreamt of."*

Incidents repeat! About two decades ago when I was born, the same Incident happened. The difference was

I was not aware of the first incident and in the second one, I was the one who had to make a choice.

That day while I was lying unconscious with a high dose of medicine, I could feel what was going around. My father came, sat near me and in the next moment wrapped me in his arms, crying. His sob was twitching me and I was so helpless that could not stop him from crying.

All he said was,

"You are my pride and property but I cannot see you suffer this way. I swore to god that each day I have been watching you.

Your symptoms exactly resemble with the symptoms of disease of your grandfather.

I tried to ignore believing that it could not be possibly repeated in you.

But it did. I lost him to Schizophrenia and Precognitive dreaming.

And now I am going to lose you... what an unfortunate father and son I am!"

And he burst out in tears!

I was not able to respond but my father's each word was absolutely loud and clear. I never knew that I was not the only one who suffered this. There was someone else in my bloodline and he was my own grandfather.

All these years I had been searching for someone who would have understood me. I wished he was alive!

For the sake of my dead grandfather, I decided to live and search for answers. This time I was not much keen to find the cure of my disease but to find answers or similar people who faced the same problem.

Maybe I had faith in my father's faith. Maybe I was not meant to die now, not this way.

Bearing pain is difficult but pushing away the pain and pretending that it is no more interfering you is even more painful.

I was paralyzed and was not able to respond to anything. Day and night I tried to fight with myself. The hallucinations that tortured me kept bothering me.

Since I was determined to live, I shifted my thought process. The first thing I did was, I destroyed *My Emerald Diary*. I saw that diary turning into ashes. Then, I decided not to stick to plans, emotions, people, incidents or accidents. I started to become forgetful. I wanted to let things flow. Those flashes kept interrupting me but I allowed it to happen like any other event in my life. I never pondered or clung to my hallucinations or precognitive dreams. It was difficult for me. Very Difficult!!

But every change is difficult.

We just need to have an attitude of acceptance!

Even today I am repellent to strong light and some smell or noises of drilling machines etc. (But I try my best to keep my mind diverted! Even today I can see images of dead people and I have unresolved questions, but I have to live and let those questions die with me.

I have stopped overthinking.

The Conclusion!

The End... with a New Beginning

Dreams touch every level of our life. They may let us glimpse the future, or give suggestions for healing, or share insights into our relationships. Above all, they can and will steer us more directly toward God.

Harold Klemp

When you are visible, everybody can see you!

This is a very true statement and it holds strong sarcasm. According to the theory of survival to the fittest, people will always find interest in everything which is tending to perfection. And that is very natural. Never blame people for that. It is the logic that is derived from science and liable to you too.

I have been attending many open mics events and other shows and I can feel that the people are expressing what they feel bad about. Heartbreaks, Betrayals, Despair... they all just want a platform to express how sad they are or how struggling their lives are. The reality is actually different. We have made ourselves so weak that we are prone to giving up. We like when someone shows care towards us. An emotional piece of art will always attract us more than a realistic one. Be it a music track or a script of a movie. We like to be consoled, loved and pampered. And as humans, our expectations are totally natural however our expectation increases when we start giving up.

You are actually stronger than what you think you are. Can't believe?

Well, I will prove with a very simple example and that is your own past. Haven't you survived that?

Never expect love from others but before that learn to love yourself.

It was too late when I realised that there was no cure to what I was suffering from because science currently have no answers to the questions for people like me.

So, I decided to cure myself.

It was not the medicines but the shift in my thought process that helped me recover. I needed counselling and hence visited many people from different realms of life, not just the 'Professional' counsellors.

The day I started taking risks, I learned to live and stay happy. It's clearly mentioned in human psychology that doing things that scare you will make you happier. **Your ultimate goal in life is to be happy and not to be just successful.**

Deflection to the Result

We often judge the correctness of a decision by the result and not by the actions taken to achieve it because of which we are always scared to step up and take risks.

As I mentioned at the beginning of the book that there is nothing like a correct judgment or a wrong judgment. They both are relative terms. Remember, perfection is repulsive and mistakes are attractive. It makes us human! So take a decision without thinking whether it will result in success or not!

When I failed, words of people were, "We knew this would happen", and when I succeeded, the words were same, just the tone was different.

I am not a broken soul …I am a mended piece... strongly mended in those areas where I was broken!

As mentioned prior, we all are used to make judgments which gradually turn into predictions. But these are often for those minds which use calculative techniques to bring out a conclusion. However, those who possess extrasensory organs can expand their consciousness which may result in connection with the outer world.

One of the profound examples is 'Dreams' and being very particular the correct terminology would be: Precognitive Dreams.

Yes, it is true that your dreams advise, console and empower you. But believe me, it's all how you take them to be!

In this vast world finding someone like yourself is very difficult however I am really thankful to the internet for letting me reach those people who faced the same problems and lived a similar life like mine.

I am sharing the experience of a writer whose name was not mentioned on the blog but he/she was the 'contributor' of **Huffington post** online portal few years ago.

"Dream-work is dualistic in nature. It is a tool for ascension here on earth and a doorway to the mysteries of the universe. Dreams emerge from the unconscious and occur in the Theta Brainwave state. I have found over the years that dream either reveal your potential or predict what is to come.

How these two possibilities manifest in dream-time is different for everyone.

As our consciousness expands, we begin to use many tools and methods to heighten awareness and bring about understanding.

One of the tools or methods is our dreams. Our nightly dreams become more significant on the path because the soul begins to use dreams as a means of communicating our progress. In this state, we are open to receive insights/information from the subconscious.

In the deeper state of Delta, our minds are passive and therefore can pick up cues from the energy of people, places, present day or future situations from what

Jung referred to as the collective unconscious.

Tapping into this collective mind is a rich source of information, guidance, and spiritual directives. Out of all your dreams, those that emanate from the spiritual realms have the most transformative effect.

These dreams are so compelling, so vivid that you cannot dismiss them and the details of such dreams remain with you for years.

These dreams are powerful in their intent to transform you, to reveal amazing and profound things about yourself and the world.

Let me mention you the names of a few known personalities who faced prophetic dreams once in their lifetime. They didn't have these dreams because they were extraordinary personalities but we know that they had these dreams because of their fame.

(Source: Rebecca Turner, World of Lucid Dreaming)

Abraham Lincoln

In 1865, two weeks before he was shot dead, Abraham Lincoln had a psychic dream about a funeral at the White House. In the dream, he asked someone who was in the casket and they replied, "the president of the United States". He told his wife about the dream but neither of them took it to heart - for on the night of his assassination he gave his bodyguard the night off.

Mark Twain

The American writer, Mark Twain, and his brother Henry once worked on riverboats on the Mississippi.

One night Mark had a dream about his brother's corpse lying in a metal coffin in his sister's living room. It rested on two chairs, with a bouquet and a single crimson flower in the center. He told his sister about his dream.

Weeks later, his brother was killed in a massive explosion on a riverboat. Many others died and were buried in wooden coffins. But one onlooker felt such pity for young Henry that she raised the money for an expensive metal coffin. At the funeral, he saw the coffin as it was in his dream. As he stood over Henry's casket, a woman placed a bouquet with a single red rose in the middle.

The Interpretation of Dreams (1899) by Sigmund Freud once again revolutionized this very human practice. Broadly speaking, this essential text gave a place to dreams that seem intuitively irrefutable. For the creator of psychoanalysis, dreams were the expression of the unconscious, of repressed desires, of our traumas and the most ignored of our emotions (which actually condition each of our thoughts and actions).

Well this topic is very controversial and left many people awestruck! It's all about the understanding of the personal unconsciousness. It is believed that if we understand our minds then we all have the potential to experience precognitive dreams. Most of us suffer from sleep induce amnesia because of which we forget our dreams and as a result we have experiences like **deja vu, gut feelings or intuitions.** People often claim that they cannot recall their dreams most of the time and that is totally normal.

There are two types of precognitive dreams, Symbolic Precognitive Dreams and Literal Precognitive. Symbolic is the one which gives you signs of some occurrence while the Literal Precognitive dreams showed the exact incidents that are displayed in our dreams. I experienced mostly symbolic precognitive dreams where I predicted deaths of few. Each dream was difficult to validate!

Dreams are never deterministic in nature. They are probabilistic so we cannot rely on them wholly. Many researches show and portray that human body is like a psychic retina which perceives photons from the future because of which precognitive dreams occur. It's not necessary that dreams occur within the spectrum of time. It may occur later than the present.

According to the theory of teleology nothing is caused without a purpose and so is the dreams. They are either desires, thoughts in subconscious minds or some flashes of events from the future.

It is believed that only ten person of our mind is used by consciousness. The person who can use more may have psychic abilities.

Writing a book on yourself is one of the easiest tasks one can do but unveiling your dark secrets and penning it down is really tough. Remembering my past brings a nervous breakdown. But again looking at the brighter side, and realising that each minute I am making a past makes me feel delighted. Today you are holding my book but this book was written in the past. And hence it is beautiful.

Success is a relative term. The more you get the more you desire, be it in the form of Wealth, Fame, Luxury or Comfort. We all live for ourselves and think for ourselves and that is great indeed and very natural.

I am gifting you this tangible part of my soul with the hope that it will help you with self-realization. I have not used many theories to explain to you, I have just used my experiences to express what I felt.

Remember there is a music within you which will be unique. You have to listen to it, dance on it and make the whole world dance with you. We cannot skip any chapter of our lives. We have to read each line and each word of the book. Feel each and every emotion of that word, meet every character. But remember, the last page of each chapter is blank and you have to write the conclusion of that chapter.

You have the world map traced in the palm of your hands... And the Universe is swirling everywhere inside the nucleus of you, electrifying the essence of who you are. You are your own archeological expedition -

Melody Lee

One day you will realize you were brave and beautiful each day of your life. I made a choice but very late. However, I believe that when you close this book after reading the last page, you will make a decision for yourself.

She cried in rains, Burned in summers

Got Scared in Storms, and fought with blunders!

Just to extract that essence of a soul which was lost in fear, doubt, and thunders.

Rising from the death was very difficult but believe me... it turned me immortal. Killing yourself is far easier, living indifferent is difficult but rising from the dead is the ultimate.

I tried hard enough to kill myself and thrice I attempted suicide because of not being heard. But, all my attempts failed!

Maybe because I had to live and that was what I was destined for.

Maybe I had to write this book and express to the world loud and clear…

Maybe I was destined to fall in love once again and once again... to dream!

Maybe I had to sing and play my guitar until my fingers bled. Maybe I had to meet You... someday!

Maybe I had to travel a long way and touch many other aspects of life… before I sleep.

I was always extremely harsh on myself because my thought process was different. I learned to forgive myself. I had my inner part buried deep inside as she was weak and ignorant. Every shadow scared her. She was a burden to me and to the world.

I thought that it was my identity but the reality is, our identity is defined by ourselves.

If you are stubborn then turn that stubbornness into your determination to achieve your goal.

If you are rigid then be rigid with your roots.

You are a perfect creation, you just need to shuffle things properly and place them in the best place to extract the incredible you.

In the process of becoming something, we consider a successful person to be the benchmark and then we strive to become like him. In this manner, we hinder our original potential and try to ape the other person.

You don't have to categorize yourself and try to be like someone. Don't limit yourself to anything. You are the decision maker of your life.

Have you ever thought about how medicines work? Well, they are not healers, they act as the catalyst to increase the healing process. A wound is healed by the hard work done by our own platelets and none other.

Freud believed that events in our childhood have a great influence on our adult lives, shaping our personality. For example, anxiety originating from traumatic experiences in a person's past is hidden from consciousness and may cause problems during adulthood (in the form of neuroses). Later I realised that my brain cannot realize the difference between reality and imagination and hence it was always stuck with confusion and mess. Only my perception could assure that difference.

Psychologically, lying requires a lot of mental effort. A person who is lying has to keep in mind, at the same time the lie – that it has to say, and the truth – in order to hide it. As a result, he uses simple sentences and finds it more difficult to cope with mental tasks. Similarly in life when you try to do what you are not meant to do, you end up messing up things and your growth is hindered.

Uneasy lies the head that wear a crown but hurdles are laid on the path of the face that wears a frown!

I tasted water, air, soil and fire, without making any judgments or without bringing out any conclusion. I let the things flow through me. Prophetic dreams were still prevalent and schizophrenia was never gone. Just the images and voices started fading as I started pushing myself to focus on other dimensions of life.

I loved to write and sing.

So I wrote my future and made a song out of it!

It was difficult to prove yourself to the world but So I never proved anything to anyone. I made them believe me.

I was never a born warrior or leader. I am the survivor. I survived where I could have given up.

I got more than twenty offer letters from organisations which many people dreamt of. But I decided to live my choice, for, I was not able to find that peace behind the glass doors and air conditioned rooms which I could have found in the open air.

I decided to pen down my experiences and share it to the world. I hope you enjoyed reading few pages of **My Emerald Diary** which I turned into ashes a few years ago, before writing this novel!

Today I have chosen happiness over 'worldly affairs' and living a peaceful life. The only difference is, my schizophrenia and precognitive dreams are living along with me!

And as Ira said to Aadir... *"believe me we will get through this...", their Sarah lived happily ... ever after!*

Love & Peace from Me to You!

Ayushi